Starcrossed

KC De la Rosa

Contents

Dedication

For my spouse, whose universe Candy and Votra started out as OCs for.
You are the reason I write romance.
And for all the baddies that need to be reminded that autistic rizz *is* real and you
have it.

Glossary of Terms

ALQEN (AL-KEN) - A planet in the Kratos galaxy. Its surface is made of aetherite, a mineral that looks like crystal. Its atmosphere is very cold. Qintaril originate from Alqen.

Daocury (dow-cure-ee) - A planet in the Kratos galaxy. Its surface is hard and rocky, and its atmosphere is very hot. Drask originate from Daocury.

Drask - An alien species originating from Daocury. They are typically dragon-like in nature, with two heads and scales of differing colors.

Drucaro (drew-car-oh) - An alien species originating from many different planets in the Kratos galaxy. They have four arms and are generally tall, six feet tall or more.

Ersea (ur-see) - An alien species originating from Medras. They are amphibian, with three vertical, oval eyes and bioluminescent skin.

Kratos Galaxy - The next galaxy over from the Milky Way, Kratos consists of fifteen planets and their moons.

Medras (meh-drahs) - A planet in the Kratos galaxy. Its surface is entirely water, and its inhabitants amphibian. Its atmosphere is temperate, leaning towards warm. Ersea originate from Medras.

Orlix (or-licks) - An alien species originating from many different planets in the Kratos galaxy. They are characterized by their pointed ears, small horns that curve up from their foreheads, and long, thin vines of darkly pigmented skin that line their arms and legs.

Qintaril (kin-tah-rill) - An alien species originating from Alqen. They are generally tall, with the average qintaril standing over 6'5". They are characterized by the keratinous horns that curve around their heads and the keratinous plates of tissue that cover the tops of their arms and legs. Their skin is generally in shades of grays and blues.

Veterok-III - The planet that Starcrossed takes place on. It is considered a hub for activity in Kratos, and is more modern in its style. The climate is varied, with its Southern hemisphere being warmer than the Northern.

Ziq'al (zee-kal) - Qin word, affectionate term for 'sibling.'

Pronunciation Guide

Votra (vah-tra)

Xyxy (zee-zee)

Jorai (juh-rai)

Yule (yoo-luh)

Qaed (kayd)

Altear (all-tear)

Zeele (zeel-uh)

Dear Reader

FIRSTLY, THANK YOU FOR picking up my book! I'm so excited for you to meet Candy, Votra, and all of their friends. Their story means the world to me.

Starcrossed is, first and foremost, a romance. A silly one. A mushy one, if you will. And also a spicy one. So, take that as your warning. There isn't much as far as triggers here, but I do want to put out a warning anyway. This book contains:

Estranged parental relationships

Cheating, past mention and off page

Injury (specifically, a plasma blast to the arm), mentioned on page but not in great detail

Penetrative sex

Content edging on alcohol abuse—it's alluded to, but not mentioned directly

As always, please take care of yourself when reading. Welcome to Starcrossed. I'm so glad you're here.

Kingsley

Chapter One

Candy

For some reason, Candy expected her first house party in space to be… different, like maybe they'd play zero gravity beer pong or something. But Xyxy's friends seemed more than happy to remain with their feet firmly on the ground. And weirdly enough, no one was playing beer pong.

Xyxy's apartment was even bigger than the house Candy used to live in with her parents and sister back home in Brooklyn. Flashing lights cycled through every color of the rainbow, flickering from every corner of the apartment, and Candy couldn't walk more than a few feet without running into one of the many side tables that were set up as do-it-yourself bars. Candy's ears pulsed with the bass-heavy music that reverberated off the walls.

Maybe a drink would be a good way to start this whole thing. She was no stranger to parties, but being at a party in a new galaxy where the only person she knew was nowhere to be found required liquid courage. She didn't recognize half the bottles of liquor lining the table closest to her, and she wasn't feeling particularly brave. The bottle closest to her was full of a sickly green liquid that everything in her human evolution warned her to avoid like the plague.

"What's your costume?" came a melodic voice from beside her. The owner of the voice was a tall, bioluminescent alien with three unblinking eyes like opals, each one fixed on her. Tendrils of tentacle-like appendages framed her bug-like features almost like hair; some more bulbous and shiny, others dotted with suckers. Her slender body was encased in a floor-length, shimmering gown a similar blue hue to her skin.

Xyxy hadn't exactly warned Candy that she was throwing a costume party the day she arrived in the galaxy, so she'd just thrown something together–her long-sleeved black off-the-shoulder top was in her regular rotation anyway, and paired with hip-hugging flared jeans completed her iconic 'Regina George gets hit by a bus' costume.

But what she hadn't considered was how she was going to explain that to a bunch of aliens who had never heard of *Mean Girls*. "Uh, it's from an Earth movie," she said, trying not to stare too hard. But she was beautiful, much more beautiful than any human she'd ever seen.

Aliens had slowly trickled their way into Earth's society, but her species was one that Candy had never seen on Earth.

"You look cute," she said, a slow smile tugging at her lips. "I'm guessing you're Xyxy's human friend? Candy?"

Figures everyone already knew about Candy and Xyxy hadn't even shown her face to introduce her around yet. "Yep, that's me." It was only then that Candy noticed the thick, glistening tail flicking languidly behind her.

"I'm Yule. I'm not sure if Xyxy mentioned this to you, but I live here too."

Xyxy had most definitely not mentioned that. Candy must have made a face, because Yule laughed. "Yeah, that sounds about right. Don't worry, I probably won't be around much. I've been back and forth to my planet a lot for work—I just forgot to conveniently not be here for this."

Candy snorted. "I should kick her ass for throwing a party my first night here. All I wanna do is get in bed."

"You wouldn't kick my ass. You love me." A pair of slender, cornflower blue arms wrapped around Candy's shoulders from behind. Tendrils of darker blue vined up the length of them from her fingertips.

Right now, she wasn't so sure about how much she loved Xyxy. But she was happy to see her. They'd had plenty of vid calls over comm since Xyxy returned to Kratos after college a few years ago, but she'd missed actually seeing her in person.

"Doesn't mean I won't kick your ass," Candy said, and Xyxy released her to stand by her side.

The best thing about this party was that she was surrounded by hot women, and her best friend was no exception to that. She was dusted head to toe with glitter, sporting a pink halter top and matching mini skirt. Her tall, chunky-heeled white boots came up to the middle of her calf. The sharp eyeliner she wore added severity to her heart-shaped face, and her silky black hair was pulled back into its usual high ponytail. She wore an earpiece that connected to a tiny, probably useless microphone that rested a few inches from her sparkly purple lips.

"Gods, look at you! You're here!" Xyxy placed her hands on either side of Candy's face. "I missed your ass so much."

Xyxy was Candy's only friend in Kratos and half the reason she decided to come out here in the first place. The decision had been an impulsive one–definitely not spurred on by a particularly messy breakup–but the chance to live with her best friend was one she couldn't really pass up. And Xyxy had been all too happy to offer her a room in her apartment. She had a job interview lined up for tomorrow, and then her life here would really begin. Candy didn't know if she would regret this or not yet, but for now she was... happy. She was having fun.

"I was just getting to know my new roommate," Candy said, sending Xyxy a pointed stare.

Xyxy's lips formed an 'o,' like she'd completely forgotten that was an important piece of information she probably should have shared with Candy. "Riiiight. Yes. Because I definitely mentioned that to you before you got here."

"You did not." Candy pinched Xyxy's side. But she couldn't even bring herself to be properly annoyed. She was just happy to be with her.

"Alright, alright, I'm being a shitty host." Xyxy looped her arm around Candy's, the most prominent edges of her nerves sloughing off at the familiar contact. "Come on, let me introduce you to some people."

"It was nice to meet you, Candy," Yule said. Candy managed a quick wave before Xyxy tugged her away and further into the apartment, where the bulk of the partygoers were gathered.

There were probably around thirty of Xyxy's friends scattered between the main living area and the dining area. Most of them were nursing drinks, chatting in small groups or dancing. Xyxy's friends were pretty unabashed in their grinding on each other. She wasn't terribly surprised, but it only added to how out of her depth she felt. Suddenly the alien liquor didn't sound so bad.

A glass shattered somewhere in the crowd, and Xyxy's pointed ears perked up like a homing beacon. "Okay, who's breaking shit?" Without so much as a glance back at Candy, she stormed into the crowd. Candy pitied whoever was about to be on the receiving end of that.

And now Candy was alone. Again. Would Xyxy notice if she slunk back to her room and hid for the rest of the night? A younger Candy might have embraced the chaos and partied until the sun came up, but fatigue pounded at her temples. Today had been chaotic enough. Road trips with her Uncle Lochlan were fun on the best of days, but her anxiety about the move made Lochlan's reckless driving all the more terrifying.

She approached one of the tables loaded with liquor and took a cup, mulling over her choices as if she had any idea what she was choosing between. She settled on the darkest liquor among them, pouring a hearty glug into the glass.

Would alien liquor even get her drunk? Surely, they had different effects on different species, right? She decided to take her chances, tipping her head back and swallowing the shot.

Which was a really fucking dumb decision.

As she swallowed, flames licked her throat, and she managed to keep her composure until a voice said, "Damn, going straight into the Daocury fire whiskey, huh?" Her embarrassment, paired with the unrelenting heat, choked her. The whiskey burned into her sinuses, making her eyes water.

A solid hand came up to pat her back, and she spluttered through the last of the liquid that traveled its way back up her throat. "Fire whiskey?" she croaked. Of all things to pick, she picked something called fire whiskey?

The stranger laughed a smooth, smoky laugh. "Yeah, fire whiskey. I'm guessing that wasn't on purpose." Candy blinked back the tears prickling at her eyes, her view of the stranger coming into focus. They were tall, at least half a foot taller than Candy, with two reptilian heads that somehow managed to look friendly despite how dragon-like they were. Most of their body was concealed by the heavy cloak that settled around their shoulders. They took Candy's glass and poured a different liquid into it; this one was concerningly thick, which didn't give her much hope. "Here. This'll help."

The fire raging in Candy's throat didn't let her argue. She sucked the liquid down and sure enough, it immediately extinguished the fire in her throat. "Holy shit," she breathed, clearing her throat. "Thank you."

"No problem." Their scaled lips on both heads curled into friendly smiles. "I'm Altear, by the way. And you're Candy, right?"

Apparently, every alien on Kratos knew who Candy was. "Wow, I'm pretty famous around here, huh?"

"Well, Xyxy hasn't stopped talking about you for the past week."

A swell of affection blossomed in Candy's chest, and she did a quick scan of the room for her aforementioned friend. Sure enough, she was ripping into who Candy assumed had broken the glass.

"Well, I hope I can live up to the hype." Candy turned back to the mini bar, which suddenly seemed even more intimidating. "What's your costume?"

Altear spread their arms to their sides and their cloak parted, revealing a deep indigo tunic that laced in the front, fitted dark trousers and a cross-strap harness lined with glass bottles filled with sparkling liquid. "You've never seen *Race to the Throne*? You know, Thuk-Dur?"

Candy did *not* know. "I'm not from here, remember?" That would be a good excuse instead of what was actually going through her mind—she was all too familiar with *Race to the Throne*, and she couldn't be less interested in the gratuitous violence and complete lack of romance.

They gasped with both heads, turning to the bottles lined up next to them and pouring themself a healthy shot of the fire whiskey. Something about this dragon-like alien drinking something called fire whiskey was amusing to her. "Okay, that's fair, but Gods, it's so good. You would absolutely love it, I can tell." They were definitely wrong about that, but Candy didn't have the heart to tell them.

They poured something into Candy's glass—a clear liquor that made Candy even more nervous. "Here, I think you'll like this. This is called cevolt. It's distilled from umdras, which is a grain that grows in Medras's oceans. It's kind of sweet but also kind of just tastes like the ocean."

They weren't doing the greatest job of selling it, but she took it, tapping her glass against theirs with a clink.

"What was that?" Altear asked.

"A cheers," Candy said. Right. That was definitely just an Earth thing. "We do it on Earth before we drink. It's like... a thing we do with friends."

"Aww, we're friends?" Altear grinned both sets of sharp teeth at her before taking their shot. They were right—the cevolt was sweet and salty. It reminded her of kettle corn, which wasn't so bad until she considered how weird drinking kettle corn would be.

"After you saved me from the fire whiskey, being your friend is the least I could do." Her head was already a little fuzzy from the back-to-back shots, but it was just enough to take the edge off her nerves. Now, she could have fun.

Or so she thought.

Next thing she knew, Altear launched into a full-blown retelling of the storyline of *Race to the Throne*. "Thuk-Dur is the underdog. He's a servant, but he has Drortall blood. He's a royal and he doesn't know it. Sorry, that's a spoiler—are you gonna watch it?"

"Maybe you can convince me?" Candy wasn't particularly in the mood to listen to the entire plot of *Race to the Throne*, but she liked Altear. They tethered her, made her feel a little less like she was floating adrift in the middle of space.

"Okay, okay, I'll just give you the notes without spoilers. So Thuk-Dur is trying to escape his life as a servant, and he makes a deal with a d'hova, which is kind of like a witch, and—"

Candy struggled to keep up; the names all blurred together, and she had a hard time keeping track of who slept with who, who ruled what country. But Altear's entire face lit up as they spoke, which anchored a part of her subconscious to the real world. She nodded along, clinging to the juiciest details, and wishing that she'd had one less drink.

Chapter Two

Votra

VOTRA LIKED PEOPLE-WATCHING. SHE had to convince herself that some part of coming to these parties was enjoyable.

Qaed had requested her presence. Despite being the more outgoing of the two, even he felt a little out of his depth at Xyxy's parties, and their thirty year long friendship meant that she had to be there with him whether she wanted to or not.

She focused now on Xyxy, ever the pragmatic host as she flitted between clusters of people, making sure everyone was having a good time while simultaneously ensuring the safety of her belongings. Votra couldn't help but wonder if she was actually having fun.

She'd been nursing the same drink for the last hour, and it was starting to become more water than liquor. She wasn't really a big drinker—but Xyxy always had nestar around; a bitter liquor from Alqen that, mixed with a little carbonated water, was Votra's drink of choice when she needed to make herself a little more palatable to the masses.

And tonight was one of those nights. The fact that she was wearing a costume only made matters worse. A couple of partygoers had asked her who she was, only for her to have to explain the intricacies of an Earth opera that no one quite understood.

Her attention fell to Qaed, who was now talking to Xyxy. He was one of many in a costume from *Race to the Throne,* and he'd explained his costume to Votra a couple of times but she simply couldn't wrap her head around the appeal of it. The black cape that fell around him like a curtain made his slate gray skin appear brighter in comparison, his silver horns curving around his head like a halo. In this costume, his broken horn looked more rugged than usual.

She debated slipping out now that he was preoccupied, but her window quickly closed when Xyxy dashed away from him. He returned to Votra's side, an amused smile playing at his lips. "Are you planning on standing there all night, *ziq'al*?"

"Perhaps. And what if I am?" Votra said, raising her glass to her lips. She wasn't planning on getting drunk—she really needed to get back to work after this, even though Qaed would probably argue with her.

He nudged her with a plated elbow. "I brought you out here to *converse.* You know, mingle. I fear you have forgotten what it is like to be in a room with anyone but yourself."

Votra dodged his prying gaze. "I am more than content on my own." That wasn't a lie. She preferred the solitude of being in her office, a sterile room of her own creation where the only thing she could hear was the sound of her own typing.

"Right, because why would the creator of a dating app need to know what it is like to make connections with others?"

Qaed was never the type to tiptoe around the subject, and he knew he was hitting a sensitive spot as soon as he brought up the app. Votra huffed out a sigh, finally meeting his gaze.

They'd grown up in the Thirteenth Ward, the smallest sector of their home planet of Alqen. Child-rearing in the Thirteenth Ward was an effort shared by every adult that lived there, making any qintaril born within a few years of each other practically siblings. Qaed was four years older than her, and from a very young age, he'd insisted on looking out for her.

Which unfortunately meant that she took his words as gospel. She gave him a pointed frown. "Do not speak logic to me," she said, draining the watery dregs of her cocktail. "I am sure I will have a conversation with someone before I leave."

Qaed gave her a look that said he wasn't impressed, but his words caught in his throat as his eyes flickered to something behind Votra. "Hm. Xyxy was not lying about her human friend."

A human? Votra had never actually met a human before. She turned to follow Qaed's line of sight. "Please, *do* try to be more obvious next time," he said.

Sure enough, a human stood by one of the bar tables, engaged in conversation with Altear. Or rather, held captive by them. She knew what it was like to be subject to one of Altear's hyper-fixation rants. It certainly took some time of knowing

Altear to find them endearing. She could only imagine what was going through the poor human's mind as Altear spoke at her.

Gods, Votra didn't know humans could look like that. All of the humans she'd seen in vids had comically long legs and torsos so thin, it was a wonder they could support the rest of their body weight. The human was only visible from behind, but Votra could already tell she looked a great deal different from the humans in the vids. She was much shorter than Votra expected, her torso thicker, curvier. Softer. Her clothes, while covering the majority of her body, clung to every slope and plane of her. Her top rode up slightly, exposing a sliver of pale skin that Votra couldn't draw her eyes away from.

"She... certainly is a human," Votra said, her chest hollow like someone had knocked all the wind out of her.

"You have such a way with words." Qaed's eyes glistened with something that Votra didn't like. "You should talk to her. She will probably be grateful to be rescued from Altear."

Votra couldn't stop herself from snorting. There was no way this gorgeous human would have any interest in speaking to her. "Perhaps she is enjoying her conversation with them."

"You and I both know that is not true." Qaed glanced quickly over Votra's shoulder. "I need to speak with Yule about something, and then we can leave, alright?"

"Of course," she said, lifting her glass to her lips but finding it empty. Maybe it was the last sip of her drink that pushed her over the edge, but she suddenly didn't feel quite so hopeless at the thought of talking to the human. She had to feel even more out of place than Votra did.

Qaed disappeared into the living room, and Votra found her eyes wandering over to the human again. Before she could talk herself out of it, she strode across the room to the human and Altear.

"—and then she killed her husband, which is good because he was trying to overthrow the king of Mordesh," Altear was saying. One set of eyes remained trained on the human, their red-scaled head turning towards Votra. "Oh, hey, Votra! I was just telling Candy about *Race to the Throne*. Have you started it yet?"

She would never escape this godsdamned television show. "No, not yet," Votra said.

Candy opened her mouth to speak—her lips were full and glossy, and Gods was it hard to stop staring at them—but Altear interjected. "I can catch you up. I was just telling Candy some of the backstory before the show starts. I read all the books, and they just don't give you all that context in the show."

Votra wasn't sure how to go about saying 'thank you but no thank you' politely, but Candy stepped in. "Maybe we can go out for drinks or something later and you can tell me about it," she said, resting a hand on Altear's arm. "I think I'm gonna make some rounds and meet some people. Like... Votra, was it?" Candy's brilliant green eyes landed on Votra, and a chill crept up the back of her neck.

"Oh, yeah, that makes sense. There are a lot of us here." Altear touched their glass against Candy's, drawing a giggle from her. What a cute sound. "Have fun out there. I'll catch you both later."

"For sure." Candy flashed her pretty, blunt white teeth at Altear in a smile. Altear left them with a raise of their clawed hand, and before Votra could edge a word in, Candy blurted, "You're the Phantom of the Opera!"

All night, Votra had wanted someone to recognize her, but now that this pretty human was staring at her with excitement shimmering in her eyes, she wanted to disappear into the floor. "I am, yes. I did not think anyone would recognize me."

"I loved that movie when I was a kid! I used to force my dad to dress up as the Phantom so that I could be Christine—" She stopped, lips pulling back in a grimace. "Which is kind of weird now that I'm saying it out loud."

Cute. Gods, she was cute. And now that Votra could see her properly, she realized that everything about Candy was adorable. Her nose turned up slightly at the end, the skin stretched across it slightly pink, just like her cheeks.

She needed a drink. She poured herself a liberal shot of nestar and topped it up with carbonated water, Candy's eyes glued to her as she did so. "It is not weird. I can only imagine you were an adorable child."

Oh, the nestar was going to her head quick. She took another sip though, fighting the urge to make a face. She'd been a little too generous with her pour. "Would you like to get some fresh air?" she asked. "I wanted to step out on the balcony for a moment. It is just... a bit overwhelming in here."

"That sounds great," Candy said, fanning herself with a hand. Her nails were the same pink as the short hair that ended just below her ears, and Votra wondered if that was a biological trait or a choice. "It's hot as hell in here."

Candy guided Votra out to the balcony just off the living room, closing the sliding glass door behind them. "God, this is so much better." She sank into one of the wrought-iron chairs, drawing her legs up to her chest and wrapping her arms around them. Votra immediately missed the little bit of skin peeking out from under her shirt.

Votra took the chair opposite Candy, crossing her legs at the ankles. "Thank you for saving us from that conversation with Altear," she said. "I have had entirely too many people trying to strong arm me into watching it, and I am just... not interested."

"Yeah, it doesn't sound like my kind of thing, either," Candy said, resting her chin on top of her knees. "I'm more of a Dr. Love's Biology kind of girl."

"Dr. Love's Biology?" Qaed gave Votra an endless amount of grief for the mindless soap opera that had taken over every second of Votra's spare time. It wasn't her fault it was addictive. "Are you caught up with the new season?"

Excitement danced in Candy's eyes as she leaned towards Votra. "Do you think they're actually gonna kill off McDreary? I mean, I heard that the actor wanted to end his contract but there's no way they can kill him while Jasi's in labor, right?"

"They have done it before. Magan left the planet right after Rinka gave birth to the twins, remember?"

"Dammit, you're right. Oh my God, they're gonna kill McDreary!" Candy buried her face in her hands, and for a moment, Votra worried that this was actually distressing her. Votra was barely coming to grips with her strange urge to comfort her when she lifted her head again. "I'm actually gonna stop watching."

"I will keep you updated about what happens if you do," Votra said. Maybe it was the fact that half of her face was covered, or maybe it was all of the nestar coursing through her, but her boldness surprised even her.

Candy didn't seem fazed. "Okay, deal."

Chapter Three

Candy

How did Candy get lucky enough to end up on a balcony with a slutty Phantom of the Opera?

Okay, maybe she wasn't slutty. But Candy definitely didn't remember the Phantom leaving the top two buttons of his shirt undone. Candy found herself drawn to the expanse of dark blue-gray skin the color of Earth's skies before a storm. She could barely make out a sliver of harder, bone-colored skin that matched the horns that circled Votra's head.

What she could see of Votra's face wasn't bad to look at, either. Half of her face was obscured by her mask, but the other half was all sharp edges. Her cheekbone was high and prominent, the slope of her face ending in a sharp, pointed jaw. She found her mind wandering, envisioning her fingers sliding down Votra's neck, across her firm chest, and even lower until—

Stop being such a creep, she told herself. She wasn't sure how long the silence that fell over them lasted, but Votra didn't seem bothered by it. In fact, she seemed happy to stare out into the night. Xyxy's apartment was in the middle of a bustling residential colony on Veterok-III, on the outskirts of a major trading hub. Candy was learning pretty quickly that this was a planet that never slept, much like her home.

Candy rose from her chair, the muscles of her ass screaming in protest. "God, I gotta tell Xyxy these chairs are the fucking worst." She crossed the small balcony to sit against the wall of the apartment's exterior. More than anything, she needed a little bit of distance from Votra.

But much to Candy's surprise, Votra moved from her chair to join Candy on the ground. Candy wrapped her arms around herself, the cool night air nipping at the exposed skin of her shoulders.

"Are you cold?" Votra asked, reaching up to untie the cape from around her neck before Candy could answer.

"A little."

Votra passed the cloak to Candy, and she knew it would probably be more practical to just use it as a blanket but she tied it around her neck as well, letting the fabric drape over her arms. "Better?"

"Yeah. Thank you." Candy knocked her knee against Votra's, and Votra didn't pull her away. Votra's leg pressed against hers felt like a hot iron against her bare skin, despite the two layers of clothing separating them.

She had to distract herself somehow. "So, you like Phantom of the Opera and Dr. Love's Biology? I'm gonna need you to tell me something really off putting about you, or I'm gonna think you're not real."

The laugh that erupted from Votra caught Candy by surprise. She tipped her head back, her laughter sharp and harsh, almost like a dog's bark. "To many people those *are* the off putting facts."

"Well, those people are wrong." There was no way Xyxy had thrown a party on Candy's first night in the galaxy, invited a hot alien who liked soap operas and Earth romance and not told her about it. Surely, there was something about Votra that was going to make Candy want to stay miles away from her.

Votra hummed in thought. "Perhaps I am a little pretentious. I take my taste in literature and film very seriously."

Candy had dated many a film bro in her day, so she was no stranger to pretentiousness. But for some reason, it was hot to imagine Votra explaining the symbolism in The Scarlet Letter because Candy was too distracted by Demi Moore's bathtub scene to care about anything else.

"Okay, give me your most pretentious take. Go ahead, make my skin crawl." Candy sat back, folding her arms over her chest. She hoped that the next words out of Votra's mouth were so annoying that her vagina dried up like the Sahara. Because right now, it was quite the opposite.

Votra took in a deep breath, and Candy found it almost comical how quickly she responded. "To preface this, I will not be upset with you if you feel the need to leave the balcony after this."

"Oh, so this is a juicy take," Candy said, waggling her eyebrows. This was gonna be good.

"I genuinely believe that anyone who regularly reads or watches romance is more emotionally intelligent than someone who believes that romance is meaningless. You are much more likely to understand the differences you might have with others if you spend your free time consuming media about loving someone for who they are despite those differences."

Fuck. Candy didn't think it was possible for Votra to be pretentious *and* hot, but she'd done it. "Okay, but that opinion's just correct," she said, drawing Votra's cloak tighter around her as if it would conceal the raging lust she was feeling for Votra right now.

God, doing this again made her feel... *alive.* Before Ross, she did this all the time. Flirting, especially. Candy *loved* to flirt. And Votra was proving to be easy to flirt with.

Votra laughed, and it was only then that Candy realized just how beautiful her eyes were–large and pupil-less, they glittered like a precious stone under the moonlight. Looking into them reminded Candy of watching the galaxies swirl past her out the window of her uncle's shuttle.

"We do not have many romance novels in Alqen. My people value action, power, money... romance is not high on our priority list. Every now and then, though, someone will publish a romance about a bounty hunter."

"Ooh, I'd read that. A sexy bounty hunter and a human, forced to work together for a common goal—and despite all odds, they fall in love along the way."

"Why a human? Are you in the market to fall in love with a sexy bounty hunter?" Votra teased.

"Hey, if it happens, it happens. I'm not closing my heart off to whatever sexy bounty hunter wants to sweep me off my feet," Candy said, shrugging.

Love was simultaneously the first and last thing on her mind. Ross had left a lasting enough impression on her dating life that she couldn't imagine opening herself up to anyone any time soon. But sitting here with Votra, allowing herself the guiltiest pleasure of getting to know someone new and being drawn to everything she learned—she loved everything about the act of dating.

Not that she was going to date Votra, of course. They'd just met, and it would be presumptuous to assume Votra would even be interested in dating a human. Maybe Votra was only staring at Candy with those exploring eyes because she thought humans were actually grotesque-looking.

"You would love *Outlaw Koran*. Koran is a former criminal who gets caught and is forced into the life of a bounty hunter, and her mark is her former partner. But then her former partner gets kidnapped by a rival crime syndicate and she has to rescue her. It is so–" Votra stopped, her cheeks flushing. All Candy wanted was for her to keep talking. "I just spoiled a large part of the movie, I am so sorry."

"No, it's okay. Keep going." Votra's voice was so pretty, Candy could listen to it all day. Hell, Votra could dictate the phone book and Candy would be enraptured.

And she did. She continued on about Koran and her girlfriend–Calypso, the criminal–and how the movie had been serialized into a book series that Votra frankly didn't like as much as she liked the movie but she still recommended because there was a lot of lore in the books that wasn't in the movie. But the book series carried on for too long. "The writers were simply drawing out the plot to make more money, I think," Votra said, and at this point, Candy would agree with literally anything Votra said.

In a sudden moment of self awareness, Votra cleared her throat. "I apologize. You came out here to get fresh air, not to listen to me ramble."

"I liked it." Candy could feel a blush rushing to her cheeks. Suddenly, being at this party didn't sound so bad after all.

Votra looked everywhere but at her. "Well, I hope that I did not hold you from the party for too long."

"I'm not really in a hurry to get back," Candy said. "I'm not gonna lie, the party's been kind of overstimulating. I literally just got to Kratos this morning and I think my brain is totally fried."

"I feel the same. I have spent my entire day at work and I am exhausted."

Candy laughed, her head coming to rest on Votra's shoulder. "When I was in my early twenties, I could be at work all day and then go out to the club until three in the morning. Xyxy and I used to go out every single weekend when she lived on Earth. But I definitely couldn't do it now, so props to you."

"Believe me, I am only here because my friend Qaed asked me to come. Otherwise, I would be asleep right now." She held one of her thick fingers in the opposite hand, brushing a finger along the underside of her hand as if soothing herself. Votra only had three fingers on each hand, but each one was probably two of Candy's.

"And you can't say no to him, huh? Xyxy's like that too. I wanted to kick her ass for throwing a party my first night here, but I love her too much."

"It sounds like she is lucky to have you," Votra said, the tenderness in her voice sending Candy's heart into a frenzy.

"Qaed's lucky to have you, too."

"He has supported me through times that no one else has." Votra's eyes flicked over to the glass door next to them. "I owe him a lifetime of parties."

"Well, I'm glad you came," Candy said, heart drumming against her ribs. She liked to flirt. She would even say that she was *good* at it. She liked to take charge of situations like this, liked to lead the conversations. But she found herself studying Votra, analyzing her every motion so that she could follow along in this flirting but not quite flirting tango they had going on.

"I am as well." Votra placed a hand on the ground between them, the tips of her fingers brushing Candy's hip as she did so.

Despite the fabric covering her hips, her skin felt hot where Votra's fingers had been. The effects of the alcohol she'd consumed were long gone, but she was still dizzy. All she could think about was how badly she wanted Votra's hands on her properly.

"Did you... leave anyone behind on Earth?" Votra asked.

Was she asking what Candy thought she was asking? "Just my family," she said, a statement that choked her up more than she intended it to. She was just trying to play coy, not lead the conversation in a completely different direction. "My parents and my sister. My uncle lives out in space. But that's it. Nothing... romantic." She looked Votra in the eye upon the last word, and Votra's dark blue lips fell open a fraction.

"I am sorry about your family," Votra said, her eyes raking down Candy's body shamelessly. Candy really regretted even mentioning her family. "Are you planning on going back to visit?"

Candy raked her teeth over her lower lip. "I'll go back later on in the year, when my uncle does. He travels for work, but he always comes back for Christmas." One thing that she was learning rather quickly about Votra was that she wasn't subtle at all. Her eyes were glued to Candy's lips; she licked her lips to test that theory, and Votra's eyes widened a fraction. "What are you thinking about?"

"I–Nothing." Her eyes darted away from Candy.

"Didn't look like nothing." She parted Votra's knees with one hand and slid between them, pinning Votra against the exterior wall of Xyxy's apartment. "*I*, for one, was thinking about kissing you."

"I would like that," Votra whispered, sliding her hands beneath the cape to rest on Candy's hips.

Candy kissed her softly at first, pulling her closer by the jaw. But when she pulled away, Votra didn't let the kiss be broken. She kissed her harder, deepening the kiss into something hungrier, more demanding. Candy gasped against Votra's lips, and Votra took that as an invitation to slide her tongue into Candy's mouth.

She hadn't been touched like this in ages. Even before she and Ross broke up, their physical intimacy had dwindled to an almost complete stop. Her heartbeat pulsed between her legs already, and she slipped a leg between Votra's. Her thigh was greeted by a steadily growing erection, and it took every ounce of her self control not to immediately dip her hand into Votra's pants.

"Do you wanna come back to my room?" Candy asked between feverish kisses, her stomach swooping as Votra's lips moved down the slope of her neck.

"Yes." Votra was already breathless, which only served to make Candy even more desperate for what was about to come.

Chapter Four

Votra

THIS WASN'T THE SORT of thing Votra did. She'd never in her life hooked up with a stranger at a party—hell, talking to strangers at parties was hard enough for her.

But now, she was letting a pretty human that she'd met maybe an hour ago lead her back to her bedroom in the middle of a party that showed no signs of slowing down. She was all too aware of the feeling of Candy's hand in hers as they weaved through Xyxy's apartment.

Candy's bedroom was tucked back in a hallway off the living room; a tiny, dark room with nothing but a bed against one wall and a dresser against the opposite one. Suitcases lined the wall next to the door. She supposed she should feel honored that Candy liked her enough to sleep with her before she'd even unpacked her things.

And she did. She felt *very* honored that someone who looked like Candy was even entertaining this with her. Honestly, Votra couldn't remember the last time someone had initiated sex with her. When she and Zeele were together, intimacy was off the table most of the time. She never turned Votra down when she propositioned her for alone time, but it always felt like she was doing it out of obligation.

This didn't feel like an obligation. Candy wanted this—her skin was hot with want as she pressed herself against Votra, capturing her lips in a searing kiss. Votra pushed Candy against the door, allowing her hands the honor of finally trailing down Candy's soft body.

"We can't have sex while you're wearing that mask," Candy managed. She reached up to untangle the string of Votra's mask from her head, her horns making it a little more difficult. "It'll ruin my favorite movie forever."

"What, do you think I will be so bad that you will remember our terrible sex every time you watch it?" Votra asked, her voice teasing, but there was truth behind her words. She was out of practice, and Candy was *incredibly* out of her league.

"No, I'm worried that I'll get horny every time I watch it because I'll be thinking about you." Candy tossed Votra's mask to the floor, her words making Votra's cock stir. "But I think it might be too late for that anyway. Every time I watch it, I'm gonna be wishing the Phantom had a few slutty little buttons undone, too." Their height difference allowed Candy direct access to Votra's slightly exposed chest. She planted slow, hot kisses on Votra's breastbone, who trembled at the contact.

"Slutty little buttons? I only had them unbuttoned because I cannot stand the feeling of buttons against my throat."

"Keep doing it. It's sexy." Candy undid the rest of Votra's buttons with urgency and pushed her shirt off her. She didn't attempt to hide the fact that she was drinking Votra in, eyes sparkling with interest. "God, you're pretty."

Votra was *definitely* hard now. She untied the cloak from around Candy's throat and it pooled on the floor at her heeled feet. The next thing she removed was Candy's shirt, and the sight before her nearly made her heart stop.

Candy's breasts were practically spilling out of her bra, a cute dot of dark pigment nestled between them. "Come here," Votra breathed, moving back towards the bed. She perched on the edge, allowing Candy to slide her thigh between Votra's. The friction against Votra's painfully erect cock drew a hiss from her.

Votra dipped her head lower to trail kisses along Candy's chest now that she could finally reach it. Her skin was soft and smelled sweet, like sugared fruit. She nipped at the sensitive skin, and Candy whimpered, pressing herself into Votra's thigh. Her hips moved against the bony plate that protected the top of Votra's thigh. She thought about letting Candy use her to get off—it felt incredible, and it allowed Votra the opportunity to focus on the gorgeous breasts that were now being practically shoved in her face.

She unclasped Candy's bra and Candy immediately shrugged it off. Greedily, Votra took both into her hands; they fit perfectly, and she swiped a testing thumb across Candy's nipple. Candy's movements against Votra's thighs increased in speed, in desperation, her hips seeking more and more friction, which Votra took as a good sign.

Gods, she looked beautiful like this. Votra was certain she could come just watching Candy ride her to her own release. "Go on, use me," Votra whispered, her voice husky with need. She bit back a groan of her own, suffocating it by pressing her lips against Candy's skin. Her mouth found those perfect, sensitive nipples, and she swirled her tongue around the bud. She pushed her thigh up against Candy, who answered by draping her arms around Votra's neck, tossing her head back as a litany of moans filled the air between them.

Candy's thighs tightened around Votra's as she came, pressing herself harder still against her as she milked the last of her orgasm. She fought to catch her breath and gave Votra's shoulder a weak shove. "Fuck, I wasn't trying to come just dry-humping your leg," she groaned, resting her forehead against Votra's shoulder. "That was embarrassing."

What was embarrassing was how close Votra was to coming in her pants. She was glad she'd managed to hold it back, because she wasn't sure she'd ever be able to face Candy again if she had. "Do not be embarrassed. I thought it was incredibly hot," Votra chuckled, gasping slightly when Candy extricated herself from her legs.

"It didn't help that I could feel you against my leg the entire time," Candy said, capturing her lower lip between her teeth. "It's kinda sexy that you got that hard just watching me fuck myself on top of you." She sank to her knees on the floor in front of Votra, pushing her knees apart and sliding her hands along Votra's inner thighs. "Can I take these off you?" She toyed with the button of Votra's pants before she had the chance to answer, peering up at Votra through thick, long eyelashes.

The sight of Candy on her knees alone was nearly enough to send Votra over the edge. "Yes, please," she breathed, lifting her hips to help Candy slide her slacks down. The thin fabric of her underwear was barely restraining her throbbing cock at this point, and when Candy pressed her lips to it, Votra balled the blanket beneath them into her fists.

Votra couldn't stop herself from moving her hips up against Candy's mouth, silently goading to move faster. The corner of Candy's kiss-swollen lips turned into a smirk as she pulled away.

Votra groaned at the loss of contact, but Candy's hands replaced her mouth, pulling her cock free from her underwear. She pressed herself into Candy's hand, not bothering to stop her impatient moans.

The head of Votra's cock was soft and flared, leading into her long, thick length roped with the same keratinous tissue that lined her jaw. The lines of harder tissue were dotted with sensitive nerves that came to life under Candy's touch.

She couldn't stop herself from sliding her hand down to tangle her fingers in that beautiful, silky pink hair as Candy's mouth finally, mercifully returned to her. Candy's tongue swirled over her slit and it took everything in Votra not to come right then.

She took Votra into her mouth—only the head at first, her hand coming up to grip the base of her cock. Candy's mouth was warm, soft, inviting, and Votra resisted the urge to push herself further into it. She didn't know how much of this humans could handle, and the last thing she wanted to do was choke her.

But Candy took her deeper, managing about half of her length before she stopped. Her hot, wet mouth stimulated the sensitive nerves lining her cock, and she laid her head back, the pressure of her orgasm blooming deep inside her.

Candy's motions on her stopped, and she pulled her mouth from Votra in a downright lewd way. "Not yet," she murmured, trailing a torturous hand along Votra's length before rising to her feet.

"Candy, please." The plea rose from her naturally. She would grovel on her knees for the feeling of Candy's mouth on her again.

Candy moved into Votra's lap, Votra's desperate, dripping cock flush against her abdomen between them. Candy was pressed against her just hard enough to send a jolt of pleasure through her, but not enough to actually quell the need.

She rose just long enough to push her jeans down her hips, revealing her thick, creamy thighs, white streaks of thin, glossy skin rippling across them. Her underwear came down next, and Candy straddled her again, her arousal hot and slick against Votra's thigh.

Votra dipped her hand between Candy's legs, and Candy cried out, her head tipping back. The moans falling from Candy's lips were delightful; ragged, demanding, Votra's name tumbling out between them. Her finger circled Candy's clit slowly, teasingly, wresting desperate moans from Candy.

But she wanted to make Candy squirm, just as she had to Votra. She withdrew her hand just as Candy's thighs started to clench around her. "Votra!" she protested between shallow breaths.

She maneuvered Candy around so that she was against the bed and moved down to rest between Candy's legs. She peppered kisses down the length of her soft stomach, selfishly taking her time. Candy's breath hitched as Votra continued her journey down her, past the thatch of wiry, curled hair, to her pussy that so desperately waited for her. Votra gave her one slow lick and Candy's moans were suddenly muffled.

Maybe she was right to cover her mouth—there was an entire party of people just outside the door. Selfishly, Votra wanted to hear it all.

Candy rewarded her with a string of soft moans once Votra's mouth was back on her. She pushed her hips against Votra's face, and Votra couldn't help but think how much she liked being buried in her.

Votra sunk the tips of her fingers into the soft flesh of Candy's thighs, and Candy hooked her legs over Votra's shoulders. All Votra could hear was the sound of her own wet, hot mouth moving against Candy, drinking her in as if she were dying of thirst. Her thick thighs clamped hard around her head, muffling everything else.

Candy's small hands gripped Votra's horns, and Votra immediately gasped at the sensation. They weren't typically sensitive, but Candy tugged on them and her cock twitched in response.

"Are you alright?" Votra murmured against Candy's inner thigh, just in case she was trying to get her attention.

"Yes, God, don't fucking stop," Candy whined, her thighs tightening around Votra again.

And she had no intention of doing so. Every new movement of her tongue sent violent shivers down Candy's body, and Votra reveled in knowing she was making her feel like this. She'd be happy to spend the rest of her days between Candy's legs.

Candy's moans grew louder, more demanding as her orgasm approached, and Votra wasn't sure how much longer she could hold out. She took her shaft into her hand, her own movements on her drawing out moans that matched Candy's.

"Are you touching yourself?" Candy asked between haggard breaths.

"Yes." Votra could barely get the word out between her own needy gasps and the movements of her tongue on that little bundle of nerves that Candy reacted so deliciously to.

"Fuck, that's hot." Candy pressed her hips up against Votra as if to punctuate her point. "Come here, I wanna see you."

Votra didn't particularly want to come up for air, but she obeyed, her hand not straying from her cock as she moved back onto the bed. Candy straddled Votra's thigh and leaned in to press her lips to Votra's. "Touch your pretty cock for me while I use you again," she whispered, and her words alone were almost enough to send Votra over the edge.

She wasn't used to being with someone who talked so much in bed… and she liked it. A lot. Candy didn't start moving against her until she started touching herself again, and a wicked smile spread across her lips. "Good girl. Do you wanna come on my tits, Votra?"

Gods dammit, she wasn't going to last much longer. She felt her lower stomach clench, her heart pounding in her ears. "Yes, I do," Votra managed between breaths.

Candy dug her teeth into her lower lip, her hips bucking wildly against Votra's thigh. "Fuck, I'm gonna come, too," she moaned, sharp fingernails of one hand seeking purchase in the flesh of Votra's shoulder. Her other slid between her legs, and heat coiled in the pit of Votra's stomach. She wasn't going to make it any longer, and honestly she didn't want to. She wanted to see Candy's beautiful, soft breasts covered in her cum.

The second the mental image flashed through her mind, every muscle in her body clenched and her cock twinged as ropes of hot, pearlescent cum decorated Candy's breasts. Candy was still riding Votra as if her life depended on it, and Votra tangled her hand in Candy's hair. She gave it a tug, testing out her theory that it felt just as good as Candy pulling on her horns. Candy's strangled gasp was answer enough. Votra tugged a little harder, revealing the length of Candy's pale neck. She pressed kisses wherever she could reach, and Candy came with a broken cry, her arousal making Votra's leg slick and sticky.

"Oh my God." Candy's entire body trembled as she moved off Votra, and she flopped back onto the mattress with a thud. "Fuck, that was good."

The sight of Candy splayed out before her, wearing nothing but Votra's cum, almost brought her dick to life again. She laid down on her side next to Candy instead, letting her eyes rake over every inch of her. "It was, thank you," she said, ignoring the wave of tenderness that washed over her.

This was why she didn't do this. Votra wasn't sure she was capable of having sex without developing feelings. This was probably the best sex she'd had in her life, and all she wanted to do was thank Candy by cooking dinner for her.

She pushed the thought away, focusing instead on forcing her body back to equilibrium. Every muscle in her lower half ached, but it was a kind of ache that she never wanted to go away.

Candy groaned, sitting up. "I should clean up," she said. She looked down at Votra and brushed her thumb over her cheekbone in a motion that was so gentle, it made Votra's heart tremble. "You can stay the night if you wanna. I know it's late."

Thank the Gods. Votra didn't know how she'd be able to drag herself out of this room, never mind all the way back home. "Thank you," she said, crawling under the covers. "I promise, I will not be in your way in the morning."

Candy opened her mouth as if to say something, but closed it a couple seconds later. "I'll be right back," she said instead, disappearing into the bathroom.

Votra stifled a yawn and buried her face into Candy's pillows. She inhaled deeply, Candy's sugary sweet smell filling her senses.

She didn't know if this was going to happen again—Candy was new to the galaxy, after all. Surely she wouldn't want to settle with the first alien she jumped into bed with.

She entertained the idea of asking Candy out on a date as her heavy eyelids finally fell closed. The last thing she remembered before sleep claimed her was Candy crawling into bed next to her, her soft body slotting perfectly between Votra's arms.

Chapter Five

Candy

CANDY REALLY WISHED SOMEONE had warned her about how bad the hangover from alien liquor would be.

Luckily, she didn't feel physically sick, but the pounding in her head was blinding. The sunlight streaming through her window only made matters worse, and she squinted against it as she tapped her comm. Veterok-III was closer to Kratos' sun than Earth was to its own sun, and she *definitely* hadn't adjusted to it yet.

Shit. Her interview was in an hour. She probably shouldn't be late, regardless of the choices she'd made last night.

She *really* needed to shower—her body still bore all the evidence of her activities from the night before. She remembered hastily wiping Votra's cum from her chest, but she hadn't been all that thorough.

The alien responsible for Candy's sticky body was nowhere to be found, but her comm flashed with a new message.

> Hello Candy, this is Votra. From last night. I got your contact information from Xyxy. I apologize for leaving so abruptly. My work mornings generally start quite early, and I did not want to disturb you. Thank you for last night. I will not forget it any time soon.

But did Votra want to see her again? She perched on the edge of her bed, gnawing at her thumbnail like it would give her the answer.

It was cute that Votra felt the need to clarify who she was, like Candy couldn't remember screaming her name all night. That had easily been the best sex of her life, and Votra hadn't even actually fucked her. The woman was so good with her tongue, she deserved an award.

She squinted against the holographic keyboard that projected above her wrist. God, it was too early for this.

> its okay! you were so quiet, i didnt even notice you leaving. i had a really good night too. i have a job interview this morning but maybe we can talk later about… a little re-peat of last night?

> also trust me, i remember who you are. very vividly.

She shuffled into the bathroom despite the pain in her head that was finally fading to a dull ache. How pathetic was it that she was kind of sad to wash the reminder of Votra off her body in the shower? *Please, get over yourself.*

She dragged a brush through her hair and dressed in a nice pair of slacks, a dark red blouse and the same heels she'd worn the night before. She didn't even really have the time to dry her hair, which probably wouldn't look the greatest, but she at least swiped a red lipstick on her lips before returning to her bedroom. She *did* still glow with that post-sex brightness that made her tired skin look perkier than it was, so that was a plus. *Thanks, Votra.*

On the way out of the room, Candy almost tripped on something, yet another reminder of the night she'd had. Votra's Phantom mask was still on the floor. She grinned to herself, picking it up and tossing it on to her bed before heading out of her room.

Until Candy deigned to buy a shuttle of her own–an expense that she *really* wasn't looking forward to–she was relegated to paying for taxi shuttles, which felt a lot fancier than they really were. Climbing into a space shuttle the size of a pick up truck but with all the sleekness of a Lamborghini made Candy feel expensive. They were *much* more spacious than the taxis she hailed in Brooklyn, and they didn't smell like old cigarettes and body odor.

Luckily, the office was in the commercial district of Veterok-III, a short fifteen minute ride from Xyxy's apartment. The building was unmarked, and only one shuttle was parked outside; it was shorter and stubbier than the taxi shuttle she'd just been in, with sun-bleached blue paint that chipped in places. Candy honestly didn't know if that was a good sign or a bad one.

If this were in New York, she would have turned and ran immediately. But she was here for new experiences, so she wasn't going to judge the creepy ass office until she walked in. And upon walking in, it was significantly less... murder-y. The reception area was empty, save for a receptionist-less reception desk and a couple of uncomfortable looking chairs lining one of the walls.

Maybe she was in the wrong place? "Hello?" Candy called, her voice reverberating through the empty room. "Is anyone here?"

"One moment!" came a voice from the depths of the office, and Candy froze.

That voice sounded so familiar, but there was no way... right? That definitely wasn't–

It *was* Votra. "My apologies, I was–" Votra emerged from a room connected to the reception room, wearing the same slacks as last night but in a maroon button-down this time. She stopped in her tracks once her dark eyes landed on Candy.

"Hi," Candy said, feeling as if all of the air had been punched out of her lungs. "You left your mask in my room last night."

Of all people to fuck at Xyxy's party, why did it have to be her potential *boss*? And why did she have to want to do it again? She still had those top two buttons undone, and Candy stole a greedy peek at her bare chest underneath.

"Did I?" Votra captured one of her hands in the other hand, trailing a thumb along the underside of it. "Um, my apologies. I did not mean to."

"It's okay." Candy took in as deep of a breath as her lungs could hold, and suddenly, her headache was much worse than it had been when she first walked in. "Uh, we don't have to do this. I'm sure you have other interviews lined up and–"

"No, please stay. If anything... this makes things a little bit easier, right?" Votra offered.

Actually, no. It definitely didn't. All Candy wanted to do was lay out across this receptionist desk and let Votra have her way with her. But something told her that wasn't something she'd be doing any time soon.

"Yeah, I guess it does." Candy couldn't help but notice Votra's eyes fighting a losing battle with Candy's boobs. She hadn't really tried to put them on full display; they were just so big, they were kind of just always there. But she liked the attention.

Votra cleared her throat. "Well, you can follow me back to the office and we can have our conversation there."

"Sure." *Be professional, Candy.* She still didn't really have the job yet, and as awkward as this was probably going to be, she still needed it. She just had to learn how not to lust after her boss. Easy.

She followed Votra through the door Votra had emerged from only a minute ago into yet another glaringly white room. How didn't this drive Votra crazy every day? The room was rather bare, save for two desks with computer terminals on them. Weirdly enough, Candy couldn't tell which one was Votra's. Both desks were completely empty.

Votra pulled the chair from one of the desks over to the other one and gestured for Candy to sit. She did, and Votra took the other seat. "Thank you for taking the time to speak with me today," Votra said primly, and Candy suppressed a smile. It was kind of cute, how hard she was trying to be professional. "You are... Candace Murdock?"

Candy immediately grimaced. The only person who called her *Candace* was her mother when she was angry. "Unfortunately. I go by Candy, though."

Votra reached into one of the drawers of her desk and pulled out a data pad, scrolling through it for a second. "My apologies, I should have had this ready. I meant to look over your work history before you came in, but my morning has been a bit rushed."

"Oh, I know." Candy couldn't help herself. She grinned, and Votra's cheeks flushed. "I can go over it for you if you'd like me to."

"Go ahead." Votra looked up from the data pad, fingers poised to take notes. "Especially share anything that is relevant to the work I am doing here."

"Well, I've never worked on a dating app before," Candy started, lacing her fingers together. "But two years ago, I helped my friends with their startup. DiversEats should be the first thing listed there. I helped develop an app that compiled locally owned restaurants in Brooklyn, organized them by price, and highlighted restaurants owned by people of color, immigrants, and queer people. I was in charge of the UI, which you should be able to see in my portfolio."

"I can, yes." Candy could see the reflection of her portfolio in Votra's inky black eyes. "This UI is incredible. Very seamless. Simple, but effective."

"A lot of apps are really busy these days, and not very accessible for people with screen readers or vision problems in general and I wanted to steer away from that while also making it look sleek and professional." Candy's chest swelled with pride. She hadn't been doing this long; it had been her quarter-life crisis pivot from what was supposed to be her career. Her degree was in nursing, but she wasn't cut out for it. She took her work home with her every day, spent her evenings sobbing over patients that she was helpless to do anything for. She wasn't the kind of person that sick people could rely on.

But making an app pretty? Piece of cake. Candy could do it in her sleep. "The next piece in my portfolio is an app that I built out entirely on my own. It was a freelance job for an online-based romance bookstore." Her lips curved into a smile. "If it wasn't based on Earth, I'd tell you to check them out."

Votra spent more time on this one, scrolling through the prototype. "Once again, very impressive." Candy couldn't help but warm under her praise. "And this is all that you had in your portfolio, correct?"

"Yeah. I'm actually pretty new to this whole thing," Candy said. "I've only been doing it for two years, but on the plus side, that means I haven't been doing it long enough to have any of my own habits. You can teach me." Votra finally looked up at her, and Candy flashed her what she hoped was a convincing grin.

Votra breathed in slowly, resting her data pad in her lap. "I have to admit, I was looking for someone with a little bit more experience," she started, and Candy's breath hitched in her throat. "But you are right. You are teachable. For only having two years' worth of experience, you show a lot of promise."

"Aww, thanks."

"My only qualm is that our timeline is very short. As you saw in the ad, we need to build out a virtual reality program within the month. That might be difficult to accomplish if I have to teach you a lot."

Maybe it came down to homosexual audacity, but Candy wasn't worried about it. There wasn't a thing in this world she felt like she couldn't nail the first time she picked it up. She could already program–how much different could creating something in virtual reality be?

"Then teach me. I'm like a sponge. I'll pick it up so fast, you'll forget that I was a newbie in the first place." Candy folded her arms under her chest, pushing her boobs up a little. Votra noticed. "You said it yourself. What I've accomplished so far is impressive."

The corner of Votra's lips quirked into a small smile. "Yes, well, that is true." She leaned back in her seat and *God,* did she look hot. "Why should I hire you over someone that I do not need to train?"

"Because I'm smart and I know that I can make an incredible product once I know what I'm doing. I'm extremely user experience focused, and that's something that you can't teach. I will make it my personal mission to make Starcrossed the best it can be for the largest number of users. I'm good at what I do. I wouldn't have applied for a job I'm frankly not qualified for if I didn't think I could do it."

Votra laughed at that, the sound much more muted than it was last night. "Telling your future boss that you are underqualified is not generally the best interview practice."

"Yeah, but being honest is." Candy propped her elbow on the arm rest of the chair and rested her chin in her hand. "And you strike me as someone who appreciates honesty."

"I do, that is very true." Votra fidgeted with her hands, not quite meeting Candy's gaze. "And while we are on the topic of honesty... I had a wonderful time with you last night. But if we are going to work together, I... cannot pursue anything further with you."

Candy's heart plummeted into her stomach, but she understood. The irresponsible part of her wanted to say fuck it, she could find a different job. She enjoyed spending time with Votra. She *really* liked having sex with Votra. Was a job really worth giving that up?

She raked her fingers through her rapidly drying hair. "Sounds like you're hiring me." She lifted a sculpted brow at Votra, who graced her with another shy smile.

"I would like to. I can send you the contract so you can look over it." Maybe she was imagining it, but she could have sworn Votra looked disappointed when she looked down at her comm to Candy's last messages.

They could have been something. Candy wanted to ask Votra on a date, a real one that didn't include sneaking around her roommate's party for some privacy. She wanted to get to know her new planet and Votra at the same time.

But finding a job was the more responsible thing to do. Her parents or Uncle Lochlan would've probably given her more money if she needed it, but she didn't want to rely on them. She needed to do things for herself.

Her comm pinged at her wrist with the contract, and Candy could feel her eyes glazing over as she read over it. It was probably a bunch of legal stuff–don't steal my work, all of your intellectual property is mine, blah blah blah. Candy was fine with signing her life away for a job, and weirdly enough, she kind of trusted Votra with it.

"Yeah, I mean, this sounds cool with me," Candy said, lazily flicking through the document. "I'm guessing you've got a 'no fucking your boss' clause in here, huh?"

Votra cleared her throat. "I believe it is on the tenth page," she said quietly, and Candy moved to the tenth page. Sure enough, there it was. *Both parties agree to maintain a strictly professional relationship for the duration of aforementioned work.* Phrased a little more elegantly than Candy would have, but that didn't make it suck any less.

"Alright, yeah. I'll sign." Candy scrolled to the bottom of the document and wrote her signature with her finger, drawing a little star at the end. She felt a bit like she was signing her vagina's death sentence–if she couldn't sleep with Votra, she *definitely* wasn't going to have time to sleep with anyone else. "There. You're legally stuck with me now."

"Welcome aboard, Ms. Murdock," Votra said.

God, now she was Ms. Murdock? She could feel her vagina shriveling already. Candy thrust her hand in Votra's direction. "Thanks, boss." When Votra looked down at her hand, puzzled, Candy said, "Sorry. This is what we do on Earth when we make a deal. We shake hands."

"Oh." Votra carefully placed her hand in Candy's, and Candy shook it. All she could think about was how badly she didn't want to let go.

Chapter Six

Votra

"So you hired her?"

Qaed's voice dripped with judgment that Votra really didn't need right now. He reclined in what was now Candy's chair, crossing one long leg over the other. It was still early in the morning, and unfortunately for Votra, Qaed's go-to when he couldn't sleep was to come and bother Votra at work. Only this time, he had an ulterior motive.

"I needed someone quickly. You know this." Votra didn't look up from her computer screen. "She was the first interview I had."

"Yeah, and every other interview you had lined up had more experience than her." He smirked, folding his arms over his chest. "I never would have pegged you as someone who thinks with her dick."

That drew Votra's attention. She ripped her gaze from the screen, narrowing her eyes at him. "I am not."

Was she? It was only then that she realized that this was a pattern. She and Zeele had only started working together because they were dating—software development wasn't even on Votra's radar at the time. But she'd learned, for Zeele. And now the tables had turned and she was going to be teaching Candy rather than having an equal to help her get the work done faster.

Her shoulders drooped. Developing an app was lonely. Ever since Zeele left, Votra confined herself to her office upwards of twelve hours a day, only taking breaks to eat and sleep. She hardly even saw Qaed anymore. Votra was prone to hyperfixation, and it tended to consume her life; her social life was at the very bottom of her hierarchy of needs.

Except for mornings like this, when she craved it, when she realized just how much she missed it. Even when Qaed was purposefully riling her up, she liked having him around. And maybe that was why she'd hired Candy.

That night had been so... easy. And that wasn't something Votra experienced very often.

"I mean, I am not saying it as a bad thing. It is about time you let yourself be lost to the throes of carnal desire."

Votra swatted at his leg. "Enough. I am now responsible for teaching her *and* getting the app ready for the launch event at the end of the month. I have enough on my plate without worrying about... *that*."

But *gods,* did she still desire Candy. If she was going to keep wearing those blouses that barely restrained her incredible breasts, Votra wasn't going to survive.

She was truly no better than a man.

"Good morning!" Candy chirped.

Shit, Votra hadn't even heard her come in.

"Good morning." Votra slipped back into Universal–it was probably a safe bet Candy didn't speak Qin, which was great considering Qaed's casual use of the phrase 'carnal desire.'

Luckily, Candy had spared Votra from the ill-fitting blouses today in favor of a silky white top under a black blazer and a skirt that was probably too short to be professional. Votra wasn't sure she minded.

Qaed honed in on her, rising from his seat–*her* seat, actually–and approaching her. "Votra did not mention how cute you were," he said smoothly, and Candy's shocked expression quickly morphed into a shy smile. "It is so nice to meet you, Candy. I have heard so much."

"Oh, you have?" Candy shot Votra a look, and she immediately wanted to disappear into her chair. "Wait, are you Qaed?"

"That depends on what you have heard about me."

To Votra's surprise, Candy immediately hugged him.

"Only good things, I promise," Candy said. She had to lift her head to look at him; while they were both small for qintaril, Qaed and Votra stood at least half a foot taller than Candy, maybe a little less in her heels. Those heels looked *really* good on her, made her already gorgeous legs look even longer.

She could tell from the look in his eyes that he was already being won over by her. Great, that was just what Votra needed–Qaed nagging her about Candy all the time.

"Hm, I am not sure I believe that." He took Candy's seat again, and Candy's eyes followed him.

"Do you not have somewhere to be?" Votra asked pointedly. She wasn't in a hurry for him to leave, but something told him that having him and Candy in the same room was a recipe for disaster. He wasn't a subtle person, nor did he attempt to be.

"No. The life of the unemployed is glorious." He folded his arms behind his head. "Just pretend like I am not here. I know you two have a lot to do."

"Kinda hard to do with you in my seat." Candy raised her eyebrows at him, and his eyes lit up with excitement. He was enjoying this too much.

He stood, gesturing to the seat with a flourish. "I was just warming it up for you, my dear."

Candy giggled, sitting in the chair and wiggling a little. "It's just the perfect amount of warm, thank you." She adjusted the seat to its lowest setting, but even still, her feet dangled a few inches off the ground. Votra definitely hadn't bought the desk chairs with human physiology in mind, and she made a mental note to buy a new one.

"My pleasure." Qaed stretched his arms over his head. "Alright, I suppose I will get out of your way. You must let me know if Votra gives you a hard time."

Votra was actually going to kill him.

"Don't worry, I will," Candy said sweetly, and Qaed swooped in to steal one more quick hug. He sent an infuriating wink in Votra's direction before, thankfully, leaving the office.

"I love him," Candy said the second the door closed behind him.

Votra snorted. "Do not tell him that. His ego does not need to be any bigger." Her comm buzzed with a message from Qaed, and an uncomfortable warmth spread through her chest.

I love her.

Ideally, she wouldn't have let them meet yet. This felt too intimate, this tangling of her two worlds. Qaed had hated Zeele from the moment he met her, and it caused nothing but trouble. They were at each other's throats whenever they had the chance to, banishing Votra to a life of mediating between her two favorite people in the world.

So it was hard not to take Qaed immediately loving Candy as a sign. Ultimately, he'd been right about Zeele. Was he right about Candy, too?

Candy drummed her pink-nailed fingertips on the arms of her chair. "Okay, boss. What's on the agenda for today?"

Right. Work. That was what they were here for. "Well, I thought that I could go over the scope of the virtual reality setup and we could do some work on it."

"Sick." Candy stood, and Votra wasn't entirely sure if that meant she was excited or not. "I'm ready to learn."

And Votra was ready to teach. She had to be.

She led Candy into the room attached to the office that she'd been using for testing the virtual reality software. She'd kept the room as simple as possible, furnished only with a bed, a dresser, and a small black rug for the purpose of testing how the software reacted to the furniture in the room. Light streamed in from a window on the opposite wall.

"My goal for the virtual reality feature is to integrate it into comms without any external hardware, so that it can be utilized in any closed room," Votra started. With a few taps on the screen of her comm, she navigated through Starcrossed to project the test VR room she'd been toying with for the past few weeks. There weren't many features yet–the projection around them turned the room into a simple but cozy bedroom, with blue satin curtains framing the single window and a rug on the floor that was more for looks than anything. The bed morphed into a slightly nicer one, with a thick, fluffy comforter that matched the curtains and at least two more pillows.

"So the VR can detect things that are actually in the room?" Candy asked, placing a testing hand on the windowpane.

"Yes. So it will transform the look of what is in the room already. Not every virtual reality room will be modeled after a bedroom. I am hoping to have some that are outside as well, to encourage casual dates without the pretense of being in a bedroom."

"So how does it work with two people in different locations?"

"One participant hosts the room, and the projection will be mirrored in both locations. The software will render the participants in a way that makes sense, as long as they are just sitting or standing rather than making any big movements."

"Got it." Candy trailed her hand along the fake curtains, her fingertips phasing through them. "How much do people have to pay for this? I mean, this is really cool."

"They are not paying for it," Votra said. She puffed her chest out slightly, preparing herself for pushback. "It is not my goal to hide any integral features behind a paywall. Anything that consumers elect to purchase will be things like premium virtual reality rooms, rooms that take a bit of extra effort to make."

"I like that." She perched on the edge of the bed, smoothing her hands over the comforter. "I can't believe you've done all this on your own. This is, like, *really* impressive, Votra."

She couldn't let herself bask in the warmth spreading through her at Candy's praise. But it felt nice to be recognized. Zeele hadn't wanted to waste time on the virtual reality aspect–it was useless, in her eyes, unless they were charging people for it.

"This is a *premium* feature" was her favorite phrase. "People would pay big money for this. We would be shooting ourselves in the foot if we let it go for free." Was Votra so wrong for wanting people to have nice things without spending their hard earned money on it?

"Thank you," she said shyly. "I fear that I have bitten off more than I can chew, but I am glad that you are here now to help."

"Yep. This is our baby now." She grimaced. "Sorry. Not our *baby*. I mean, I guess there are *worse* babies that could come from a one night stand...." She stopped. "Not that babies are bad. I don't hate babies. I'm not a *monster*."

Candy was so cute, it was starting to piss Votra off. If she managed to survive this month without kissing her, she'd be proud of herself.

"Shall we get to work?" Votra opened the door for her and led her back into the office.

And now, they were going to work. And that was it.

Votra leaned over the back of Candy's chair once she sat, leading her through the different programs used to code the virtual reality features. She had to admit, Candy was every bit as smart as she claimed to be in the interview. She soaked up Votra's instructions like a sponge. She didn't have to repeat herself once.

Though, she did end up repeating herself because the position she'd put herself in proved to be very distracting. She could see directly down Candy's shirt, and a good half of her brain power was occupied by reminding herself not to look. And somehow, she'd developed a Pavlovian response to the sugary smell of Candy's perfume. She was half-hard and Candy was hardly saying a word.

"So, how do you feel?" Votra asked. "Do you think that this is something you will be able to handle?"

"Oh, definitely. I got this, don't you worry."

"Good." The tiny hairs lining Candy's neck stood at attention, and Votra let herself revel in having that effect on her for just a second before she moved away. "So I will probably have you work on the design for some room elements and build out the framework for them. Is that alright?"

"Hey, you're the boss. I'll do whatever you want me to," Candy said. She knew what Candy meant, but she'd be damned if the words didn't go immediately between Votra's legs. *Gods, get yourself together.*

She relegated herself to her own seat, forcing distance between them to keep her dick under control. "We are a team now. I am not necessarily your boss. If there is anything that you think is not working or anything that can be improved in any way, I expect you to tell me."

"Really?" When Votra looked up, Candy had turned in her seat to look at her, her eyes a fraction wider. "Are you sure?"

This was a strange change of pace. Starcrossed, back before it was Starcrossed, wasn't Votra's at all, despite the fact that its inception had been her idea. Everything was Zeele's, and Votra's opinions were generally brushed off. And she'd grown used to that. No matter how long she'd worked on it, no matter how much of her time she'd put in, she would probably let Candy railroad her if she felt the need to.

"Yes. I am but one set of eyes. Surely, there are things that you will find that I have missed."

"I doubt it. Starcrossed is really amazing, Votra, and I'm not just saying that because you sign my paychecks." Candy grinned, and Votra's heart thrummed in her chest. "Not that it means much coming from me. You have way more experience than I do."

But her opinion did matter, maybe a little too much. "I appreciate that," she said quietly, turning her attention back to her computer. "It does mean a lot. I have put years of my life into this, and I fear the whole thing is starting to blur. It is difficult to be objective about it."

"Well, objectively, you did a great job." Votra wasn't looking at Candy, but she was painfully aware of her eyes on her. "I just hope that my work can be on par with yours."

"I am not concerned," Votra said. She'd been working up to this, this relinquishing control, placing what felt like her life's work into someone else's hands. Showing Candy Starcrossed's code felt like laying her soul bare in front of her, and strangely enough, she trusted her with it. She wasn't sure there was much she wouldn't trust Candy Murdock with.

Chapter Seven

Candy

CANDY DIDN'T KNOW WHAT she expected when it came to working with Votra, but what she learned pretty quickly was that Work Votra was *very* different from Party Votra. They didn't talk much, save for Votra thanking Candy every time she brought her coffee. She strictly spoke to Candy only when she needed something or when she was showing Candy how to do something. And as much as she knew she shouldn't be thinking about it, her heart went crazy every time Votra leaned over the back of her chair to look at her computer screen.

It was her third day of work when Xyxy sent her a comm message. Votra's hand was on the back of her chair, and Candy was so focused on how incredible Votra smelled that she almost missed the text message. She smelled smoky but sweet, like the strong brewed Thai teas she used to get back home.

> ur going on a date tonight, fyi

> okaaaaay with who??

> hes one of qaeds friends… friends? idk how he knows him but qaed said he was single so

> what do you know about him??

> hes a film dude, i know you like those film dudes

> and hes actually pretty hot. his names dren

> ur meeting him at laika at 7

Well, at least Candy didn't have to do any of the work. And honestly, she could use the distraction. She hadn't been on a date in years—a date that wasn't with Ross, anyway, and those barely counted. They weren't really dates; they were more Candy being held hostage for two hours while Ross talked about whatever film he was working on and lecturing Candy for saying the word 'movie.'

But tragically, her attraction to the creative types never waned, no matter how shitty a lot of them could be.

She got home from work two hours before her date, which gave her more than enough time to get ready. God, she didn't even remember how to get ready for a date. With Ross, it didn't really matter what she wore. He never seemed to notice—she'd had to point out her newly bubblegum pink hair to him when they went out the night after she'd dyed it.

But those days were over, she reminded herself. She was gonna go out with someone who was going to notice her, someone who was going to compliment her outfit and maybe let her get a word or two in during dinner.

But she also had every intention of looking so hot, her date could do nothing but stare at her. She layered a black camisole under a white tie-front blouse, shoving her tits up to her neck with her smallest bra. Her skirt fell to her ankles, with a slit that reached her mid-thigh.

"You can do this, Candy," she told herself, staring into her own green eyes in the mirror. "You're gonna have a good time and you're not gonna think about Votra or work." She was in a brand new galaxy, after all. She'd never lived anywhere but New York, and she should be taking this time to have new experiences, not being hung up on her boss.

Laika was a glamorous but casual restaurant in Veterok-III's commercial district, nestled on the corner of a street. Outside, the tables overflowed with young aliens enjoying meals of vibrantly colored food; the air hummed with conversation and the warm, spicy aroma of a food that Candy didn't recognize. She lingered outside the restaurant, her comm buzzing with a message from an unknown user.

> Hey, this is Dren! Xyxy passed me your comm info. Just letting you know I'm running a little late. Grab us a table and I'll be right there!

Being late on a first date wasn't exactly the greenest of flags, but she didn't exactly have the best idea of what traffic on Veterok-III was like, or how traffic even *worked*. God, she needed to get out more.

She gave him the benefit of the doubt and obliged, following the host to a secluded corner table bathed in the soft glow of pink-orange moonlight streaming in through the window next to it. She peered out the window; one of Veterok-III's moons bared its warm face to her, taking up a much larger portion of the sky than Earth's moon did.

Her heart quickened at how intimate the setting felt. *It's just one date with one guy, Candy. You're gonna be fine.*

The waiter, a kind-faced ersea with skin the color of algae, had been over twice to check on Candy by the time Dren arrived. He already wasn't doing so great in Candy's book, but first impressions weren't always right. The least she could do was give him a chance.

And anyway, Xyxy had been right about the fact that he was hot. He was a tall orlix with brick-red skin and fiery orange hair clipped close to his head. At least he'd dressed nicely—his pinstriped slacks fit him well, and his white linen button-up hung about his thick torso loosely, the top two buttons undone. The last time she'd seen someone with two buttons undone like that, she'd felt a lot more tempted than she did now.

"Traffic was nuts, you wouldn't believe it," Dren said, taking his seat across from Candy. "I hope you weren't waiting for too long."

She was, but there wasn't much she could do about it now. "I figured I would wait for you before I ordered anything. Are you gonna get a drink?"

"Probably. They have a pretty big selection of spirits from outside Kratos. If you've never had a zyphar fizz, you should definitely try it." Dren placed his hands on top of the menu, pupil-less topaz eyes settling on Candy. "So, you're from Earth, right? How are you liking Kratos so far?"

"I haven't seen a lot of it yet, honestly. I've been working a lot, so I haven't had the chance to see much. But it is pretty cool to be somewhere brand new. I was born and raised on Earth, so...." She cleared her throat. "What about you? Are you from here?"

"Yep. Born and raised on Veterok-III, so I can be your tour guide whenever you want. I can show you all the places only the locals know about." Dren grinned. *See, your first impression of him was wrong. He's nice!*

"I'd like that," Candy said, looking back up at their server as she approached the table again.

"I'll take a zyphar fizz," Dren said, his eyes flicking down to his comm. He didn't look up at the server as he continued. "And can we please have an order of fried thryska for the table?"

"I'll have a zyphar fizz too, please," Candy said. "Is everything okay?"

"Yeah! Sorry. My friend is texting me about our show. I don't know if Xyxy mentioned it to you or not, but I'm an actor. And writer... and director. Not to brag or anything," he said, flashing her a fanged grin when he looked back up at her. As Dren spoke, his eyes twinkled, and a wave of warmth washed over Candy. This was what got her. She couldn't resist the pull of someone talking about their passions, even if it meant that they didn't want to hear a word she said.

Their server returned with their drinks, and Candy thanked her before she hurried off. "So you're writing a show?"

"Well, writing it *and* directing it. My friend is taking the lead role and he's gonna help me–" He looked back down at his comm when it pinged again. He abandoned his sentence as he started to type back.

This time, he was silent for a while. Candy drummed her fingers on the table.

Unfortunately, she was all too used to this. Ross used to do the same thing—he was practically glued to his phone, especially when he was waiting to hear back about auditions. This was what she got for always going after film bros. She would always come last, apparently.

Dren looked back up as if surprised that Candy was still there. "Shit, sorry. There's so much going on in my brain right now." He took a sip of his drink and let out a gasp of satisfaction. "What do you think of the zyphar fizz?"

She took a careful sip, and the bitter taste immediately exploded across her tongue and filled her mouth. It wasn't immediately off-putting, but she definitely didn't enjoy it. Apparently, she wasn't great at muting her facial features, because Dren laughed a full belly laugh at her. "Don't worry. One day, your palate will become refined enough to like it."

She slid it towards him. "You can have it if you want." Maybe he'd pay more attention to her if he was a little tipsy.

Their server returned with their fried thryska, which almost reminded Candy of calamari. The plate was piled high with what almost looked like fried tentacles, an array of brightly colored sauces circling them.

The thryska was much better than her drink. It had an almost meat-like texture but practically melted in her mouth, the softness offset by the crunchy, fried coating. "Oh my God, that's good," Candy sighed. At least, even if the date sucked, she'd discovered some Kratos food that she liked.

"Right? Try the green sauce. It's the best one," Dren said. She wasn't entirely sure that she trusted his taste, but she followed his lead, dunking a sliver of thryska into the sauce. The sauce was creamy and vegetal, and honestly, she thought the thryska was better without it. But she didn't particularly want to hear Dren's critique of her taste buds, so she kept it to herself.

Dren's comm let out a series of beeps, and once again, he was lost to his conversation with his friend. Candy let out an irritated sigh, and Dren either didn't care about it or didn't hear it. She snacked lazily on the thryska between them, and by the time Dren looked back up at her, she'd nearly finished the entire plate. His loss.

"You know what? I really need to call him real quick," he said, his eyes on her looking genuinely guilty. "I'm so sorry. I told him I was going out tonight, but this is something that I really have to handle."

Candy knew that she shouldn't take this personally, but she was. She knew his type. He was a fledgling screenwriter/director/whatever the fuck he wanted to call himself who thought his not-quite career was more important than everyone around him. She couldn't help but think that, if he was really sorry, he'd deal with this later.

But maybe she was being selfish. "It's fine," she said, waving him off. "Take your time."

"When the server comes back, can you order the spicy craukvek for me?"

Was he really going to be gone that long? But Candy acquiesced and nodded. She'd gotten good at this over her time with Ross. This was no different.

But why would she come out here to date someone who was exactly like Ross? There was a reason they hadn't worked out—aside from the whole cheating thing.

The minutes Dren was gone slowly turned into half an hour, and Candy had already ordered her food and picked at it for a few minutes by the time she looked down at her comm again. She wanted to be polite and wait for him, but her food was getting cold.

She asked the server for her food to go and left the table in favor of the bar. Something told her Dren had already forgotten that she existed.

A long bar lined with seats ran through the middle of the restaurant—a perfect hiding spot. Candy took a bar stool on the opposite side from where she and Dren had been sitting. The bartender, a golden-skinned drucaro wielding four cocktail shakers, gave her a questioning look. "That bad, huh?" she asked, skillfully pouring a milky blue substance into a glass.

"Yep." Candy's eyes prickled with irritated tears. She hated that she cried when she was angry. All in all, this wasn't the *worst* date she'd ever been on. Was she dumb to have expected better?

Or maybe she was just expecting too much out of men. "Do you have any Earth liquor?"

The drucaro chuckled. "We work with a distillery based on Earth–but we just have tequila. That okay?"

Now Candy was *actually* going to cry. "I could kiss you right now."

The bartender poured her a shot and slid it to her. Typically, Candy would take her shots with lime and salt, but she tipped the shot back without thinking twice. It burned in a way that made her feel like she was home again.

Maybe coming out here was a bad idea. There had to be a reason that all of this was going wrong.

Or maybe it was just her. She'd been so convinced her whole life that love was easy. It was for her parents—they were so disgustingly in love, Candy had no reason to assume it wasn't like that for everyone.

But she'd learned pretty quickly in her adult years that it definitely wasn't like that for everyone. In fact, it might just be them.

"Can you give her one more and then close her out? I will pay," came a voice from behind her, forcefully yanking her out of her self-pity. Votra was standing beside her, cradling a container of food.

"You want anything, Votra?" asked the bartender, and Candy's eyebrows shot up to her hairline. Votra didn't seem like the type to be a regular at any restaurant, never mind one as nice as Laika. Hell, Candy hadn't so much as seen Votra eat the entire time they'd worked together.

"I am alright, thank you. I am going right back to work after this." She tapped her comm to the bartender's, and the bartender slid Candy another shot.

Just when she thought things couldn't get any worse, they did. The last person Candy wanted to see her like this was Votra. What cruel god had placed her in a room with the only two people in the galaxy that she had ever been remotely interested in?

"You didn't have to pay for my drinks, y'know," she grumbled. Her second shot went down much easier than the first.

"I know." Votra's eyes on her were infuriatingly soft. "What happened?"

"Nothing." Candy slid off her bar stool, looking everywhere but at Votra. The thought of her boss seeing her after a less-than-perfect date set her nerves on edge. "I'm leaving now."

She didn't know where she was going. She sure as hell didn't wanna go home and face Xyxy, because she knew that as soon as she found out how the date had gone, she'd make a huge fuss over her. And honestly, Candy just wanted to pretend none of this had happened.

"Wait." Votra's large hand circled Candy's wrist, stopping her in her tracks. "Would you like to come back to the office with me? I have a bit of work to do and I could use the company."

"Yeah... okay. Thanks," she said, her voice brittle.

Chapter Eight

Votra

CANDY FOLLOWED AT VOTRA's heels as they headed into the office, curling into her chair as Votra sat at hers. She tossed her food container onto her desk and wrapped her arms around her legs.

"What are you eating?" Candy asked, resting her chin atop her knees.

"This is finke. Laika is one of the only places outside of Alqen that I can get it."

Candy rolled her chair over towards Votra's. "Can I try?"

Votra extended her fork towards Candy, expecting her to take it, but Candy opened her mouth instead. Her cheeks warmed as she fed Candy, the gesture so intimate it made her stomach twist.

Candy's eyes flew open wide as she chewed. "Wait, that's so good," she said. "What's in it?"

A quiet pride swelled within her at Candy's words. "It is ce'qil simmered in a sauce made of algra and some other spices. Ce'qil is sort of like... a root vegetable? And algra is an herb—that is where the bitter flavor comes from."

Candy took the fork from Votra, popping another saucy chunk of ce'qil into her mouth. "Any chance you wanna share?"

Something told her she couldn't really say no, but she wasn't sure she wanted to. "It seems like we are already sharing," she pointed out.

"Good point." She passed Votra's fork back to her, leaning her elbow on Votra's desk and propping her head up on her hand. "Thanks for paying for my drinks back at the restaurant, by the way. Sorry I was being weird."

"You were not being weird." Votra's attention shifted from her food and she rested her fork in the creamy green sauce. "What happened, if you do not mind my asking?"

Candy huffed out a sigh. "Xyxy set me up on a blind date and it kind of sucked." She stabbed a piece of ce'qil rather aggressively with the fork. "I think he said all of about five sentences to me before he disappeared to take a phone call. He probably doesn't even know I'm gone."

"He just disappeared?"

"Yeah. He's a big movie guy and he was talking about how he's working with someone on a show and apparently, this phone call was more important than being out with me." Candy pushed a chunk of ce'qil around in its sauce. "Sorry. All this just brought up some weird feelings. It's a stupid thing to get worked up about." Votra suppressed the urge to do *something* to comfort her. "I mean, I get it, I guess. When you're chasing your passion, you never take days off. You're on, 24/7. You probably feel like that, right?"

She did. She wasn't sure she'd turned her brain off once in the last five years. "I suppose I do," she said.

"Would you have taken a work phone call on a date?"

Votra wasn't good enough of a person to say that she wouldn't. "I unfortunately have before, which does not make me much better than your date," she said, taking her fork back from Candy to take a bite. "But in my defense, working with your significant other generally requires work conversations on dates."

Candy's jaw stilled as she stopped chewing. "You worked with your significant other?"

"Yes." Votra swallowed. "My ex-girlfriend and I created Starcrossed originally. But that was a long time ago and a lot has changed since then."

"I'm sorry. It must be weird for you to work on it without her." She leaned her elbow on Votra's desk and placed her chin in her palm. "Did you break up because of work?"

"Something like that." She pushed the container of finke towards Candy. "Would you like the rest?"

"You don't want anymore?"

"No, I am full. I would hate for it to go to waste." Thinking about Zeele had turned her stomach, and she wasn't sure she could force another bite past her lips. Being in the office was permanent enough of a reminder that Zeele had once been the cornerstone of her life; the last thing she wanted to do was think or talk about her.

"Thank you." Candy slid the container closer to herself, taking Votra's fork from her. "I never worked with my ex, but I think we would've broken up a lot earlier if we had."

"It is hard, combining your work life with your personal life. You start to forget where one ends and the other begins." Votra swallowed back the lump forming in the back of her throat.

"Ah. The 'no fucking' clause in my contract is starting to make sense now."

"It is not a... 'no fucking' clause." Votra's voice grew small, and she felt her cheeks grow warm. "It is, more specifically, a 'no relationship' clause."

"I get it." Candy's voice grew softer, and she closed the container of food after taking her last bite. "I promise, no hard feelings. I shouldn't be thinking about relationships anyway. I just got out of one and I think my brain is still trying to get itself together."

Votra's stomach swooped uncomfortably. "Was it a bad one?"

"Bad enough that my first logical thought was to move a galaxy away from him." Candy shrugged a shoulder. "I really thought that I was over it. You know, when you can tell a relationship's days are numbered and you start mourning it before it's over? That was me for the last, like, year of our relationship. I had a feeling he was cheating on me and I just ignored it until I came back to our apartment and there was literally another girl in our bed."

"Gods. I am so sorry," Votra said quietly. She couldn't imagine the desire to cheat on *anyone*, but especially not Candy. One night together and she had consumed Votra's every waking thought. She couldn't imagine sparing a thought on anyone else.

"It just undid all of the work I'd done to get over him, you know? I freaked out and I ran away." Candy's eyes grew misty, and she rubbed them with the heel of her palm. "Tonight brought up a lot of that. The guy I went on a date with was nice, but he just kept ignoring me for his comm. And Ross used to do the same thing. I got so used to being unimportant, and I could feel myself going back to that place with Dren."

Votra's chest grew tight, and she couldn't stop herself from reaching out to push a lock of Candy's hair from her face. "I am glad that you left. You do not deserve to be treated like that by anyone."

"I know, right? I deserve to be *flaunted.*" Candy finally grinned, which Votra took as a small victory.

She was right. She *did* deserve to be flaunted. And Gods, did Votra wish it could be her who did it.

"I am sorry you have had such a bad night," Votra said, rising from her seat and offering a hand to Candy. Candy took it, standing from her seat with a little groan. "If I may... I know something that might help you."

"Okay."

Votra guided her into the virtual reality room and tapped a few buttons on her comm. Within seconds, the room around them transformed into a bedroom that had slowly become more familiar to Votra than her own.

The small bed became an elegant four-poster, with curtains that draped around it. A few candles flickered from the now stone walls, casting a warm, mellow light over the room. A fireplace crackled from the wall opposite the bed, which immediately drew Candy's attention.

"Ooh, the fireplace is new," she grinned, reaching her hands out towards the fire as if it might actually warm her. "You did this one all by yourself?"

"Yes." Votra perched on the edge of the bed, wedging her hands between her knees. "I come in here to think sometimes. The office can be a bit much."

"I get that. It feels very... work-y." Candy sat cross-legged on the floor in front of the fireplace. She stuck her hand into the virtual flames, wiggling her fingers around and seeming quite pleased with herself. "But this room looks like something out of an old romance novel."

Votra felt her cheeks warming. "Well, yes. I imagined what Juliet's bedroom might look like, but then I realized that a bedroom modeled after a tragedy might not be the most peaceful."

"You really liked Romeo and Juliet, huh?" Candy blinked, whipping her head around to look at Votra. "Oh my God. Is that where Starcrossed came from?"

"Yes." Votra's cheeks warmed.

"That's so cute." Candy stood, crossing the room to approach the bed. She attempted to lean against one of the posters, but she phased through it and stumbled. Without thinking, Votra leaped to her feet and steadied her with two hands bracketing her hips.

A blush crept up from Candy's neck all the way to her cheeks. "The virtual reality in here is so good, I forgot it wasn't real," she said sheepishly. "Sorry."

"It is alright. I am glad you did not fall. These floors are quite hard." Votra didn't move her hands, no matter how much she knew she should.

"Are you saying that out of experience?" Candy teased, those pretty green eyes locked onto Votra's.

Votra's heart rocketed into her throat. It wasn't as if she hadn't been this close to Candy before. But bathed in the warm glow of the candles around them, the fireplace illuminating her from behind... Votra swallowed hard. "I am. In the early days of developing this, I did a lot of what you just did."

"But you didn't have a big, strong woman to catch you when you fell."

Zeele wouldn't have tried. She laughed, the few times it happened when she was in the room. "You think I am strong?" Votra asked, a bemused smile touching her lips.

"I mean, you *did* just jump up and catch me like some kind of superhero." Candy slid her hands up Votra's torso, letting them rest on her chest.

Votra had never really been considered *strong* before. As far as qintaril went, Votra was pretty small. She was relatively lean and only six feet tall. Even her younger sibling was nearly half a foot taller than her.

Her skin grew hot where Candy's hands rested. "I only did what I had to do," she said.

It would be so easy to kiss her. She was right here, her face practically level with Votra's chest. She just needed to lean down a little, and–

Candy beat her to it. The kiss was immediately rough and needy, Candy's blunt teeth scraping against Votra's lower lip. Votra couldn't keep herself from groaning against Candy's lips, and her body moved faster than her brain could, hands seeking out Candy's waist to tug her closer.

This wasn't right. Candy was only just recovering from her bad night. "Candy," Votra breathed against Candy's lips. Her mouth struggled with the words she knew she should say. She'd spent a lot of time thinking about sleeping with Candy again—more time than any boss should spend thinking about their employee. And none of those dream scenarios included Candy being miserable after a bad first date. It just didn't feel right.

Candy faltered, wrenching herself from Votra's grasp. "Shit. Sorry. I'm... in a weird place right now."

Votra deflated. "You had a hard night. You have nothing to apologize for."

Candy cleared her throat and stepped back, eyes flicking towards the door. "I should probably get home. It's late, and I've held you up enough already."

"Of course." Votra chewed her lower lip. "Do you need a ride home?"

"No, it's okay. I'll grab a taxi." In a move that surprised Votra so much she was sure she'd stopped breathing, Candy rose onto the balls of her feet to press a kiss to Votra's cheek. "Thanks for taking care of me tonight. It means a lot more to me than I can tell you. And I'm sorry, again."

Votra didn't want Candy to feel sorry about anything ever again. "It was my pleasure. Get some rest tomorrow."

Because Candy was off tomorrow, and Votra would be at the office alone. Again.

"You get home soon too, okay?" Candy said.

"I will." But once Candy left, Votra couldn't bring herself to do much more than sink into the bed that looked a lot more comfortable than it was. She hadn't spent the night in the office in a long time, but maybe tonight would break that streak.

Chapter Nine

Candy

THERE WERE SO MANY things Candy could do with her day off, and she had gone to bed with every intention of doing them. But when she woke up, all she wanted to do was go into the office.

Who was she? The old Candy Murdock *never* sought out an opportunity to work more than she absolutely had to. But then again, she probably wouldn't get much actually done if she went in. Actually *being* around Votra would probably be torture.

God, she should have taken the chance to jump Votra's bones last night when it presented itself. It would have been so easy. She was *right there.* Damn her for being considerate of Candy's feelings.

So instead, she shoved herself out of bed, got dressed, and took herself on a walk to a little breakfast restaurant not too far from the apartment. She used to do things like this all the time–before Ross, anyway. Dating herself was her favorite thing to do.

She chose a table outside on the restaurant's patio, allowing her to watch the shuttles whizz by as she sipped her drink. Her cocktail was a creamy, cevolt-based drink, which she remembered from her conversation with Altear at the party.

Her comm pinged on her wrist, and a message from Votra popped up.

> Letting you know before I forget, I am reworking some of the code for the virtual reality rooms we have been working on. I tested one of them this morning and the bed was not rendering correctly.

This was probably an update that could've waited until Candy came back to the office tomorrow. A sneaky, hopeful part of Candy wondered if Votra was using this as an excuse to open a line of communication with her.

And of course, Candy fell for it.

> youre the best!!! you sure you dont need me today? i can come in. youre doing so much on your own

> Of course not. I told you I would not work you over forty hours, and you have already surpassed that. I will be alright here without you for one day.

> aww so you dont miss me?

Candy's message was met with a silence long enough to let her order something that sounded an awful lot like a waffle but probably wasn't one. She'd only just started to wonder if she'd scared Votra away when another message came in.

> The office is a lot quieter without you here. That used to be a good thing, but it feels kind of strange now.

That message had a *way* stronger impact on her than it should have. Her cheeks tingled with warmth, and she placed her hands against them in a vain attempt to cool them.

> i could come over there and make it REAL loud in there... if you know what i mean ;)

> jk lol

She absolutely was *not* joking.

> I should get back to work.

Yikes. She was about to give up when another message came through.

> Thinking about how much I want that is very distracting.

Candy choked on her drink. Who *was* this? She chewed her lip, pondering how she wanted to play this. She didn't want to scare Votra off, but she *definitely* didn't want to put a stop to it.

> youre the one that messaged me first so really you started this

> if you didnt wanna be distracted you shouldnt have messaged me

So now you are pushing the blame off on me?

I was simply messaging you about something work related. It was not my intention to turn it into something else.

> ooh, does that mean this is turning into something else?

What would it be turning into?

> i mean it almost sounds like ur trying to sext with me

…I am unfamiliar with that phrase.

Of course she was. How convenient.

> its like… when u talk about sex over comm messages

> but unfortunately i cant do that, i signed a no sexting contract

I do not believe that your contract has a specific 'no sexting' clause in it. It is hard to write a clause banning something that you did not know existed.

> are u telling me sexting is allowed?

All I am saying is that it is not NOT allowed.

Oh my God. Votra all but said 'please sext with me.' That was exactly what was happening here. Candy squirmed in her seat, fingers poised over the holographic keyboard as she planned her strategy.

Sexting with other people had been so easy. In fact, Candy kind of loved it. But when it came to Votra, she found herself overthinking it. Votra deserved a good sext, a *quality* sext.

> okaaaay so if i tell you i havent stopped thinking about your cock since that first night, that's okay?

> Candy. Please.

God, Candy wished she could hear Votra actually saying that.

> is that a no?

> No, it was not.

> It is more than okay. I would not be opposed, even, to you going into detail.

Holy shit. Was she really sexting with her boss right now? Xyxy would be so fucking proud of her for this.

Candy nearly jumped out of her skin when the server placed her food in front of her. The dish in front of her smelled delicious. It almost looked like a crepe, shaped into a roll and stuffed with some sort of cream and a blood-red fruit.

Focus on your food, you horny monster. She shoved a forkful into her mouth, chewing over how she wanted to play this.

Votra had *literally* made her wait to sign her contract until she agreed that they wouldn't sleep together again. But last night had *definitely* happened, and this–whatever this was–was definitely happening, too.

It wouldn't hurt to push it and see how far it went, right?

> your dick is genuinely the prettiest dick ive ever seen in my life

> Go on.

It took all of Candy's self control not to squeal. Her words immediately brought to mind their first night, when she rode Votra's deliciously ridged thigh like her life depended on it. Shit, she was supposed to be riling *Votra* up, not herself.

i love that youre demanding me to keep praising you

even sucking your dick felt amazing. human dicks dont feel anywhere near as good as yours did

In what way?

the RIDGES. votra do you even understand that you are every human with a vagina's dream

i just know that riding your dick would be fucking incredible

Votra was silent for a while, and for a moment, Candy thought that she'd pushed it *too* far. But Votra's next message nearly sent Candy out of her seat.

Imagining you on top of me has me so hard I can hardly concentrate.

show me? :3c

If Votra was going to draw the line somewhere, it was here. And for a moment, Candy thought she was going to.

But mid-bite a few minutes later, Votra sent a picture–a mild one, but a picture nonetheless–of her clothed erection. *Oh my God, I have to get out of here.*

votra, i am in PUBLIC

You literally asked for this.

gimme a second, i need to get out of here

Why?

because i want you to tell me what you would do if i was there and i cant read messages like that in public

Well, that worked. Votra didn't answer until Candy got her food boxed up and paid for her meal, giving the waitress a generous tip just out of principle. *I'm sorry I sexted at a table in your section, here's 30%.* Candy wasn't even sure tipping was a thing on Veterok-III, but the server deserved it anyway.

> You know, it was kind of cruel to start something you could not finish.

> and what are you gonna do about it?

Candy bolted into her room the second she got home, locking the door behind her. She crawled into bed and reached into her bedside table for her bright pink vibrator. Damn, she should have bought a blue one.

> Are you home yet?

Aww, she was impatient. Candy grinned.

> yep, im in my bed. waiting

> i think you were gonna tell me something

> About how I would push you against the wall and kiss down your neck with my thigh between your legs?

Fuck. Warmth blossomed between Candy's legs, and she rubbed her thighs together hungrily.

> good girl. what else?

> I would slide your skirt down and kiss down your thighs.

> would you kneel for me?

> Please, yes

Candy would never get tired of this, of Votra being putty in her hands even when she wasn't anywhere near her.

> you would look so pretty on your knees for me

> i would slide my panties off and put my leg over your shoulder so you can taste me

I would love to taste you.

Are you imagining that now? My face between your legs?

Well now she was. She turned her vibrator on, kicking her shorts off and trailing the head over her dripping wet pussy.

Fuck, she wished she had just gone to the office so Votra could do all these things to her instead of just telling her about them. But it was fun to imagine Votra in her chair, cock in her hand, wishing for the exact same thing.

> yes

> sadly my vibrator isnt as good as your tongue

Are you touching yourself, thinking about me?

> yes

Fuck

> are you?

Yes

> you gotta give me more than one word answers

It is difficult to concentrate on messaging you when I need you this badly.

Need. Candy liked to be needed. She kicked her panties off, moving the slick plastic against her throbbing clit. She didn't know what it was like to be fucked with Votra's gorgeous, ribbed dick, but it was all she wanted. She whimpered at the slow vibrations against her, her breathing turning ragged.

> are you thinking about fucking my mouth with your pretty cock

> i like choking on you

> I want you to taste me, too

> ooh, you want me to swallow huh

> youre so fucking hot

> you taste so good

And now all Candy could focus on was the thought of Votra releasing her load all over her face, into her mouth... her stomach swooped dangerously as she lined the vibrator up with her entrance. She was already more than lubricated enough, her pussy practically weeping with need.

> after you cum in my mouth im gonna put my hands on you and get you hard all over again so you can fuck me

> i wanna be filled by you

> You are going to be the death of me, Candy Murdock.

> oh i like you using my full name

> do you have a last name

> wait dont answer that right now tell me how hard youre gonna fuck me

> I want you on top of me, so that I can watch you take every inch of me.

Candy physically couldn't stop the moan that filtered past her clamped shut lips, and she pushed the vibrator in further, the smaller head vibrating at her clit while the longer one brushed against her g-spot. Every muscle in the lower half of her body clenched, sweat prickling at her hairline as her orgasm swelled inside her.

Votra would look so good under her, those giant hands on her hips, trailing over her stomach, cupping her tits and brushing her thumbs over her nipples. Candy's toes curled and she whimpered out Votra's name, physically unable to force herself to send back a message. Her comm vibrated again just as her orgasm crashed over her, her toes curling and her walls pulsing around the vibrator.

God, she hadn't come that hard in a *long* time. Or maybe ever. She slipped the vibrator out of her with a shudder and dropped it onto the bed next to her. She could deal with that later.

Her body shivered with the aftershock of her orgasm, and she peered down at the last message.

> Also, I do not have a family name. Qintaril do not have family names like humans.

> hmm, good to know

> fuck, i just came so hard im dizzy

> sorry, thats probably not sexy

> Believe me, it is.

> It is definitely sexier than me telling you how embarrassingly quick I was.

> really? when did you come?

> Somewhere between my 'pretty cock' and 'you taste so good.'

Something about that was endearing. Candy was *really* starting to have fun with this glaringly obvious praise kink Votra had.

> actually thats

> stupid hot

> i like that you get off to me telling you how good you are

> its just so fun to tell you how much i like your dick

I am begging you not to start again.

> i also like it when you beg

I am silencing my comm now because I cannot afford to do this again. I am quite off track now.

> i could come in and support you from under your desk while you get back on track

Goodbye, Candy.

...And also, thank you. I do enjoy being distracted by you.

A knock at her door dragged Candy from her nap. Shit, when had she fallen asleep?

"You alive in there?" came Xyxy's voice from the other side.

She still bore all the evidence of what she'd been up to before she fell asleep; her panties and shorts discarded on the floor by the foot of the bed, vibrator used and forgotten on the bed next to her. "Uh, yeah!" she called back. "I'm... naked. I just showered."

"Oh. Can I come in?" Candy should've known that wouldn't faze her. This wouldn't be the first time Xyxy had seen her naked, but it would *definitely* be the first time she'd seen her post-nut. And she wasn't sure their friendship was ready for that yet.

"Not yet! Hang on!" She scrambled out of bed and kicked the underwear under it. That was a problem for tonight's Candy.

Shit, did it smell like sex in here? Candy couldn't tell. She tugged on a pair of pajama pants that she found on the floor and opened the door a crack. "What's up?" she asked as coolly as she could.

Xyxy's eyebrows crept up her forehead. "You good in here?" she asked, peering over her shoulder as if she'd see something.

"Yep! Fantastic, actually," Candy said. "Uh, you need something?"

"I was gonna invite you out, but it looks like you're in the middle of something?"

Not anymore. Candy cleared her throat. "No, no, I'm good! I can go out! What were you thinking?"

Xyxy absolutely didn't seem convinced. "Girls' night. You, me, and Yule. Unless you're too busy."

A girls' night *did* sound really nice. Plus, she'd only encountered Yule a handful of times in the week they'd lived together.

"I'm not! Just, uh, give me some time to get ready." What time was it, even? She felt like she'd slept for days.

Xyxy's eyes finally landed on exactly what she was looking for. "Girl, you could've just told me you were jerkin' it in there," she snickered. "You know I'm the last person who's gonna shame you for that."

All of the heat in Candy's body rushed to her face. Shit, she forgot to put the vibrator away. "Was it at least good?" Xyxy asked, eyebrows raised.

"God, yeah it was." The answer escaped Candy before she could even think about it. She dropped her voice low, opening the door a little wider and leaning towards Xyxy. "Me and Votra were *sexting*. I've literally never sexted with anyone in my life."

"Okay, bitch, move. I'm coming in." Xyxy forced her way into the bedroom, shutting the door behind her. She hopped onto Candy's bed, sitting criss-crossed. "Tell me everything."

Candy didn't know that she could look Xyxy in the eye while she recounted the *ridiculously* hot sexting that had made her come so hard, she'd taken a three hour long nap afterwards. She moved to her closet, rummaging through her clothes for something to wear tonight.

This was far from the first time she'd told Xyxy about her sexual escapades, but it was definitely the first time she'd told Xyxy about a *good* one. Sex with Ross almost always left much to be desired, and she could count the number of times he'd actually made her orgasm on one hand. In a week, Votra had made Candy come more times than Ross had in five years.

Candy wondered for a second if Votra would be proud of that. She should be.

"I mean, Votra's pretty shy. I don't know that she'd want me to tell you *everything*," Candy said. Ross probably also didn't want Candy telling Xyxy just how shit he was in bed, but that hadn't stopped her before.

Xyxy was uncharacteristically quiet for a moment, the room filled with only the metallic scraping of coat hangers against the rail. "You like her, don't you?"

Candy took a dress off its hanger. She hadn't worn this dress in *ages,* and she wondered for a second if it would even fit her. She snorted dismissively at Xyxy's question. She didn't like Votra... did she? "Trust me, I'm not in any place to be liking anyone, *especially* not my boss."

Xyxy made a noncommittal noise as she rose off the bed. "Doesn't mean it can't happen." She trailed her dark red-painted nails over the fabric of the dress. "Oh, shit, this one's good."

"Right?" Candy sloughed off her pajamas and tugged the dress on, Xyxy occasionally stepping in to spot her. The dress clung to her like a second skin everywhere except the sleeves, which draped loosely over her shoulders. She could immediately feel the dress constricting her ribs, but she *knew* she looked good.

Xyxy gave Candy's ass a firm slap. "I am *obsessed* with you. Okay, I'm gonna go tell Yule to get ready." She paused, placing a hand on Candy's cheek. "Just be careful with Votra, okay? I don't wanna see you getting hurt."

Xyxy's outlook on romance had been pretty dire for a few months now, since her divorce was finalized. She'd stayed tight-lipped about the whole thing, and Candy still wasn't exactly clear about what happened, but whatever it was had clearly left its mark on her. Candy pulled Xyxy in for a tight hug, relishing this rare display of emotion from her best friend.

"I'll be fine, I promise," Candy said. God, did she hope she was right. "I love you. Thank you."

"Okay, okay," Xyxy said, immediately squirming from Candy's grasp. Honest conversations about feelings never lasted very long with Xyxy—Candy liked to be an open book, but prying genuine feelings from Xyxy was like drawing blood from a stone. "Put some makeup on, you horny freak."

Chapter Ten

Candy

CANDY WAS EXCITED TO be seen out in public with her two hot roommates. Xyxy was in a simple but effective two-piece set, composed of a halter neck top that was corseted down the middle and a skirt that was somehow even shorter than Candy's. Yule was dressed a little more conservatively, though Xyxy's influence was pretty obvious. She wore a lilac dress that accented the pretty, pearlescent blue of her skin, with long, billowing sleeves and a deep cut that exposed a swath of bare skin.

"I'm buying your drinks tonight," Yule declared, looping her arm through Candy's once they climbed out of the shuttle taxi. "You're not allowed to let anyone else buy drinks for you, okay? No matter how hot they are."

"Right. Tonight is for *you*. We're gonna spoil you and you're gonna have a great time." Xyxy grabbed Candy's cheeks and pressed a solid kiss to her forehead. "I love you. I'm sorry last night sucked ass but tonight is gonna make up for it, I promise."

Honestly, last night hadn't even been that bad. Her time with Votra had definitely overridden the sour taste Dren had left in her mouth, but who was she to deny her friends' gifts? Free drinks and all of their attention on her was exactly what she needed.

It took Candy a second to recognize the commercial district that she'd been in just the night before. Xyxy led them to a club on the busier side of the district, a massive building that stretched across half of the upper level. An archway of gleaming neon lights marked the entrance, a line of club-goers wrapping around the building.

But Xyxy wasn't fazed. She strode past the line and approached the bouncer, a crimson skinned drucaro with an even darker red mullet and four arms thicker than Candy's head. "Jorai, my beloved," Xyxy sang as the bouncer was letting in a group of aliens in flashy silver bodysuits. "I was hoping you were gonna be here tonight."

"How convenient," Jorai said, draping a set of arms around Xyxy's waist as Xyxy dropped a kiss to her cheek. Both sets of dark, pupil-less eyes curved into crescents as she smiled. "You're gonna get me fired if you keep skipping my line like this."

"Yeah, but... I brought Candy." Xyxy fluttered her mascaraed eyelashes at Jorai, and all four eyes landed on Candy.

"Oh shit! You're Candy?" Jorai didn't drop her hold on Xyxy as she thrust a hand out towards Candy. "You guys shake hands on Earth, right?"

"Sometimes." Candy grinned, shaking the black nailed hand offered to her. "It's a little formal for meeting a new friend but, uh, good for you for knowing."

"Humans are so weird." Jorai glanced over Candy's shoulder to Yule, who looked remarkably uncomfortable. "Hey, Yule."

"Jorai." Yule breezed past Jorai and let herself into the club, eliciting a snicker from Xyxy. Candy couldn't wait to hear what that was all about.

Jorai's arms around Xyxy dropped. "Okay, go on in before you piss off everyone in this line," she said, ushering Xyxy and Candy into the club.

As they walked in, the overwhelming bass of the music hit them, and Candy squinted against the strobing lights as her eyes adjusted. Xyxy made a beeline for the bar, Candy following her and Yule joining them shortly after.

"Can I get three shots of cinqos, please?" she shouted against the music.

Candy and Yule leaned against the bar on either side of her. "What's the deal with you and Jorai?" Candy asked Yule, leaning across Xyxy to make herself heard.

Yule's immediate look was one of disgust. "We slept together once and it was a terrible experience."

That Jorai? Candy couldn't endeavor to understand how someone with muscles the size of her head and four massive hands could be bad in bed. "No way."

Xyxy immediately downed one of the shots that the bartender gave her, passing the other two to her friends. "Come on. It wasn't that bad."

"Do I need to remind you that she called out someone else's name while I was literally *inside* her?" Yule clicked her tongue with irritation and tipped back her shot. She hated to say it, but Yule's story was making her feel better about her own dating life. She took her shot as well, pleasantly surprised to find that it was actually pretty decent. It was almost cinnamon-y, with a warm spice that lingered at the base of her throat.

Candy grimaced. "Was it her partner's name or something?"

"Nope." Yule ordered another round of cinqos. "She's just... really hung up on someone."

Candy couldn't help but notice Xyxy squirming a little, taking her shot the second it hit the bar.

"And now our poor, sweet Yule is relegated to the life of lusting after a gay man," Xyxy sang, earning her a smack from Yule's long, slick tail.

Candy couldn't believe she'd missed out on all of this. She expected a certain degree of messiness from Xyxy, but not Yule.

"Wait, who? Do I know him?" Candy asked, going through her mental rolodex of people she'd met since moving here.

Yule took her shot in lieu of answering, then pushed herself away from the bar. "I'm gonna go dance."

"Without me?" A dark gray arm slid around Yule's shoulder, an arm attached to a very drunk looking Qaed. His cheeks were flushed and his big, dark eyes were glassy. Yule stiffened so visibly under his touch that Candy could see it despite the darkness of the club.

Oh my God. The gay guy that Yule was in love with was *Qaed*? This poor, poor girl.

"Get your drunk paws off my girl," Xyxy said, swatting at Qaed's muscular arm. Qaed answered by pulling her closer, and Yule looked like she wanted to melt into the floor.

Candy couldn't blame Yule for being flustered. Qaed looked *hot*. His muscular torso was barely contained by the skin-tight black crop top he wore. Fashionably baggy black cargo pants hung off his sharp hips.

"I was just saying hello," Qaed said, raising his free hand in surrender. "I did not know that you three were coming tonight."

"Candy had a really shitty date so we're having a girls' night," Xyxy said, and Candy shot a frown in her direction.

Qaed cocked his head. "Your date with Dren did not go well?"

Candy narrowed her eyes at Qaed. She'd totally forgotten that this was very much *his* fault. "Just wondering, have you ever met the guy? He's kind of unbearable."

Qaed answered her with a grimace. "I have met him... maybe twice?"

She was actually going to kill him. "Okay, well do everyone in your life a favor and stop setting people up with him. He's a *terrible* date."

"Shit. Okay, understood. Sorry, Candy." He peeled himself away from Yule, giving Candy's forearm an apologetic squeeze. "Let me buy you another drink. It is the least I could do."

"You can buy us *all* a round," Xyxy said with a flutter of her long lashes.

Qaed snorted. "You were just as responsible for Candy's shitty date as I am. You are not getting a free drink." He followed Candy to the bar, but honestly, she wasn't sure she was ready for another drink. She was already starting to feel a little fuzzy, and if she got actually drunk, she might find herself saying something she'd regret later. She was, however, just tipsy enough that thinking about Votra for a second turned into the overwhelming desire to talk about her in general.

And she needed that to go away. She ordered herself another shot of cinqos and Qaed tapped his comm to the terminal at the bar. "You know, if you will accept my opinion on something else... I know someone else who might be good for you," he murmured, leaning his shoulder into Candy's. God, he reeked of alcohol.

She downed her shot and put her shot glass back on the counter a little harder than she intended to. "Yeah, I don't know exactly how much I trust your opinion right now," Candy said.

"Okay, fair." He raked his teeth over his lower lip. "For what it is worth, though, I think you and Votra would be good together. Gods only know she needs someone who is not also married to her work." The alcohol-induced warmth in Candy's cheeks rushed to every other part of her body. "She talks about you a lot. I have not heard her talk about someone so much in a long time. A *really* long time."

Candy swatted him away. There was no way Votra actually talked about her. "We *do* work together. It makes sense that she talks about me a lot." It was hard to imagine Votra having a conversation with anyone that *wasn't* about work. That had to be all it was.

Qaed moved away from Candy with a shrug of his shoulder. "Just an observation. Enjoy your girls' night." Yule watched him particularly closely as he disappeared onto the dance floor, and Candy rested her hands on her hot cheeks.

Votra talked about her? To Qaed? What kind of things was she saying? She wasn't allowed much time to spiral; Xyxy grabbed her hand and dragged her into the crowd, Yule following behind them.

Candy let her thoughts be lost to the rhythmic pounding of the bass-heavy music in her ears. Xyxy's hands found Candy's hips, and she grinned, allowing herself to revel in the wave of affection that washed over her. Her best friend was hot, the strobing lights reflecting off her sharp features. Candy draped her arms around her shoulders and leaned in close. "Thanks for taking me out," she said, just loud enough to make herself heard over the music. "I love you."

"I love you more." Xyxy kissed Candy's cheek. "I'm so glad you're here."

Candy was glad, too. Yule joined them once Candy pulled away from Xyxy, and Xyxy moved her hands from Candy in favor of grabbing one of Yule's. Candy took her other hand, and in that moment, she wasn't sure she'd ever been happier. She'd missed this. A lot. When she was dating Ross, she hardly had the time to spare to go out with her friends. He kept her on set until late into the night, and the few times she *did* go out with her friends, he always had something to say about it. About how she should've been with him instead, how he needed her more than her friends did.

But the truth was, Candy needed *them*. She'd dug herself into a hole of loneliness that only Ross could pull her out of, and even then, he was all too willing to let her sink back into it when it was convenient for him. Xyxy was her only constant, calling her every night even when she wasn't free, and she loved her for it.

After a few songs, Candy needed a break. When had she gotten so out of shape? She used to be able to go all night, but they were only about five songs in and Candy's lungs were on fire. She weaved her way off the dance floor and headed for the bathroom for just a few minutes of reprieve.

She was just about to go into the bathroom when she spotted a familiar figure out of the corner of her eye. Qaed braced his back against the wall, head tipped back slightly.

"Hey, you look like shit," she said, resting a hand on his upper arm. "You okay?"

"I am fine." He didn't exactly *look* fine. "*Totally* fine. More fine than I have ever been, in fact." His words slurred together more than they had earlier.

Her eyebrows crept up and she rested her hands on her hips. "You don't look fine. Jesus, how much did you drink?"

"Too much."

"Yeah, I gathered that. Come on, I'm taking you home."

"I do not know if I can move away from the wall without falling over." He giggled to himself, pushing off the wall as if to test his theory. And, true to his word, he wobbled violently and Candy grabbed his thick forearm to steady him. "Hm. Yes. I was right."

Candy huffed. Xyxy and Yule wouldn't be much help–Qaed was easily over two hundred pounds of dead weight. "Hold on. I'm gonna go get Jorai and call Votra to pick you up."

"*Noooo,* not Votra. Anyone but Votra." He screwed his eyes shut, and for a moment, he looked like he might actually throw up. And Candy *really* didn't want to be here for that. "Just shove me in a taxi, I will be fine."

What a pain in the ass. "I'm not shoving your drunk ass in a taxi. I'll come with you. Just... stay there. Don't move."

"I could not even if I wanted to."

This wasn't exactly how she'd planned on her night going, but she couldn't just leave him. Not Votra's best friend. She retrieved Jorai from the front door and recruited her help to bring Qaed out of the bar. He shifted all of his weight against her, but she hardly seemed fazed. She walked him out of the bar like it was nothing. Candy *really* hoped that the fresh air would sober him up a little.

"God, you're strong," Candy said, at which Jorai grinned.

"I'm a wrestler. I gotta be." She propped Qaed up against the bar's exterior wall. "You doin' okay, bud?"

"I am fantastic, thank you." His eyes were slightly less glassy than they were inside, which put Candy at ease. "You do not have to come with me, Candy. You should stay with your friends."

"You're my friend too, unfortunately, and I gotta make sure you get home safe." She rested her head against his arm. "Jorai, can you tell Xyxy and Yule where I went? I told them I was just going to the bathroom real quick."

"Ooh, Jorai would *love* to talk to Xyxy," Qaed grinned, his head drooping to rest against Candy's. God, even his *head* was heavy.

"Don't listen to him. He's drunk."

"Hey, as her best friend, I think I've earned the right to ask questions," Candy said, her knees buckling under Qaed's weight. Xyxy would sooner die than tell Candy what was going on in her life, so Jorai was possibly her only hope. "What *is* the deal with you two?"

"Nothing! We're just friends," Jorai said. She opened her mouth to speak again just as the taxi pulled up. Dammit, there went her chance. "C'mon, let's go." She looped her arms around Qaed and hoisted him into the back seat of the taxi.

"Thanks for your help," Candy said, giving Jorai a brief hug before climbing into the taxi. She was going to have to get the story another day. Jorai shut the door behind them and Qaed immediately laid all of his body weight against Candy as the taxi took off.

Without the filter of the alcohol-soaked air of the bar, Qaed smelled like a bar mat. But she let him lean on her anyway. "If you throw up on me, I'll kill you," she muttered.

"No promises." His eyes fluttered closed, and she hooked her arm around his. Poor thing. Candy hadn't gotten as drunk as Qaed in *years*–once she hit twenty-five, the hangovers just stopped being worth it.

Her comm buzzed, a message from Votra appearing on her screen. Shit, she should probably tell Votra what was going on. If she knew Votra, she was probably still at work, and the last thing she wanted to do was distract her.

> Do you mind coming in a bit early tomorrow morning? I discovered a bug with the virtual reality interface that I would like your feedback on, and I have a feeling it will not be an easy fix.

This *would* be Candy's luck. She groaned, and Qaed let out a groan in response that she was pretty sure was meant to be mocking her. Maybe she should've just thrown him into the taxi after all.

> ill try but no promises. your best friend is passed out on me rn

> Wait, what? Qaed?

Before Candy had the chance to explain herself, Votra called her. Candy tapped her comm to answer. "Hey."

"What is going on?" Votra sounded nervous. "Is Qaed alright?"

"*Nooo,* I told you not to tell Votra." Qaed leaned into Candy's comm. "I am fine, do not worry. Candy is prank calling you. I am not drunk."

"Qaed, you are not supposed to be drinking this much." Votra sighed, her voice crackling through the comm. "Where are you?"

"We're in a taxi right now. I'm gonna take him home and get him into bed. I might stay with him."

"There is no need. I will be there." Votra's voice was suddenly small. "Thank you for taking care of him, Candy."

"No problem." Candy glanced out the window to see the shuttle coming to a stop. "Oh, I think we're here. How long before you get here?"

"I am already here. I will come down and help you with him."

What was Votra doing at Qaed's apartment? "Okay, cool. See you in a second then." Candy hung up and got out of the taxi after paying the driver. Qaed seemed a little less out of it when she rounded the taxi to his side; he managed to force himself to his feet with Candy's help, and he wobbled in her grip as she helped him onto the sidewalk.

The apartment complex stretched out in front of them in a wall of doors; there had to be at least ten floors of them. Candy *really* hoped they wouldn't have to go up many steps. Her own legs were turning to jelly, and she couldn't imagine how Qaed was feeling.

"You holding up okay, champ?" she asked him, holding him around his thin torso.

"Ask me again after we get up the stairs." He started towards the first set of stairs, and Candy followed his lead. Just before they reached the steps, Qaed let out a groan. "Dammit, you called Votra?"

"*Yes,* Qaed, you were there." Candy looked up just in time to see Votra descending the stairs in a large t-shirt and baggy pajama pants. She'd be distracted by how cute she was if she didn't look so stressed. She launched into what Candy could only assume was very spirited nagging in a language that Candy didn't understand. Qaed shrunk against Candy, and Votra pulled him from her grip.

"I can take him from here. Thank you." Votra's tone was clipped, and Candy flinched against it. She must have noticed, because her voice softened. "I am sorry that you got dragged into this. You should get home."

"Let me help." Candy took Qaed's opposite arm. "I don't know if you know this or not, but this guy is dead weight."

"Hey!"

Votra smiled. "Thank you."

Candy and Votra lugged Qaed to his apartment–up *four* flights of steps and down one more–and by the time they reached the door, Candy felt like she was going to pass out, too. Every muscle fiber in her body screamed for rest.

Votra took him to his room, and Candy took the liberty of plopping down on the couch. It would just be for a minute, she told herself. She was going to have to prepare herself for the journey back down those stairs. God, why would Qaed subject himself to living somewhere like this?

When Votra came back out of Qaed's room, she seemed surprised to see Candy still there. "I am sorry again that you had to do that," she said, tucking a leg under herself as she sat on the couch next to Candy.

"No, it's okay. I didn't wanna just leave him there." Now that Votra seemed more relaxed, Candy let herself appreciate how sweet she looked in her oversized pajamas. The Votra Candy saw every day was always dressed so sharply, in a way that only accentuated her harsh features. But this Votra looked... soft. "Are you gonna spend the night with him?"

"Well, I live here, so I do not have much of a choice."

That explained a lot. "Oh. Right."

The corner of Votra's lips curved into a smile. "Would you like something to drink? Some water?"

Candy had never needed water so badly in her life. "Yes, please."

Chapter Eleven

Votra

THERE WAS TOO MUCH going on in Votra's head, and for a moment, she felt about as drunk as Qaed.

She was frustrated, mostly, that he'd gotten *this* drunk again and Candy had gotten roped into it. But at the same time, she was happy to see Candy, especially in the dress she was wearing.

She gave her a glass of water, which she drank half of immediately. "Ugh, thanks. I needed that. I haven't drank this much in a while and I swear I can already feel the hangover starting." She placed the glass on the coffee table, resting her pink head against the cushion behind her. "Is Qaed okay?"

"He is fine. He is probably already asleep." This dress was *really* good on her–the hem of the skirt had ridden up her thighs as she sat down, and Votra was torn between tugging it down to preserve her modesty and hiking it up around her hips.

"Are *you* okay?" Candy poked Votra's leg with her heeled foot.

Votra exhaled, pinching the bridge of her nose. "I am, yes. I just worry about him. I have told him to be careful with how much he drinks, and he just does *not* listen. He needs to be careful, after what–" She stopped, clearing her throat. "I wish that he would take better care of himself."

"He's lucky to have you." Candy reached for one of Votra's hands and held it between her two smaller ones. "You're always looking out for him. That has to be stressful."

She wasn't sure if it was the feeling of Candy's hands enveloping hers or the fact that she was coming down from a rush of adrenaline, but she suddenly felt like crying. "He is my brother. I have to worry about him."

"I didn't know you two were related."

"We are not by blood. But we grew up together. My parents raised him. He took care of me when we were young, and I am trying to return the favor. But he is stubborn and does not like to accept help." She drew in a deep, shuddering breath, and Candy squeezed her hand. "I know that he is going through something and he will not open up to me about it. He does not have to speak to me about everything going on in his life, but... I wish that he would talk to me about this, whatever it is."

Candy drew their joined hands to her mouth and brushed her lips across Votra's knuckles. "I get how you feel. Xyxy's the same way. She acts like everything is totally fine, but she isn't really herself. I guess I just have to trust that she's going to come to me when she's ready. Just like Qaed will."

"I hope that you are right." Votra let her eyes settle unfocused on their hands. "I did not mean to put all of my problems on you."

"It's okay. I'm glad you're opening up to me." Candy brushed her thumb across the top of Votra's hand, and she could feel herself finally relaxing. "I like learning about you. As hot as the whole tall, dark, mysterious thing is... I wanna know who you are."

Votra's heart stuttered. Why? Why would someone like Candy be interested in *her*, of all people? "I feel the same about you. You are fascinating to me." She pulled her hand from Candy's but reclaimed one of them, trailing a large fingertip across the pad of Candy's hand. Candy shivered against her touch, but didn't pull away.

Votra wanted to make her shiver again. She trailed her fingers up the length of Candy's arm slowly, leaving goosebumps in their wake. Up until now, Votra's thoughts were static. Loud, distracting, thrumming painfully in her ears. But touching Candy grounded her, and the only thought in her mind now was how badly she wanted to touch her more.

A shy smile tugged at the corners of Candy's lips, and it only made the urge to kiss her stronger. "We gotta stop getting handsy with each other the second one of us has a bad night," she said, resting a hand on Votra's knee.

"That does not have to be a bad thing," Votra murmured. She'd been so starved of touch for so long, and Candy was so generous with it that she was growing addicted, fast. Her soft hands were the balm she didn't know she needed until they were upon her, smoothing away the stress bundling her nerves like she was smoothing the wrinkles out of a blanket.

Candy's eyes on her grew soft, her thumb brushing across the fabric of her pajama pants. "There *has* to be a time that's more right than this."

Votra would be lying if she said she hadn't imagined the perfect scenario–coming home from a date, maybe, without her drunk brother passed out in the other bedroom. Without Candy crying over a bad date. Without the pretense that they weren't supposed to be doing this.

"What if the timing is never right?" Votra asked, her voice strained. "No time in the next two weeks is going to be *right*. And then what? Then you and I stop working together and we never see each other again?"

Candy froze. They hadn't talked about what came next. Votra was afraid to. She wouldn't blame Candy for not wanting to see her afterwards. They'd already spent at least sixty hours a week together for the last two, if not more. Gods only knew Votra wasn't easy to be around that long.

"I don't want that to happen," Candy whispered, her eyes glistening with unshed tears. "I don't know what's next for us, but... I don't want this to be it." She leaned in, cupping Votra's jaw in one hand. "The one thing I know is that I can't sign another contract with a 'no fucking' clause. Not with you."

"How many times do I have to tell you that it is not a 'no fucking' clause?" Votra smiled despite herself, and Candy finally laughed, a sound Votra had been so desperate to hear. "I think I can permit a breach of contract. Or two."

"How generous of you." Candy climbed into Votra's lap, draping her arms around her neck. "Can I kiss you?"

This was it. There was no turning back from this. She was officially opening the door to... whatever this was. This thing that she'd built up so many walls to protect herself from, that she'd taken legal measures to prevent from happening.

And it only took Candy Murdock two weeks to break them down.

"Please," she whispered, and Candy immediately drew her in for a slow, careful kiss. A kiss like she might break Votra if she kissed her any harder.

But maybe Votra wanted Candy to break her. She was so good at maintaining her put-together facade, at mastering what was expected of her–eye contact, confidence, a careful, measured way of speaking because the tangents she often got off on were unprofessional.

That wasn't her. That wasn't who Votra was. And maybe she wanted Candy to see that.

She deepened the kiss, her tongue seeking entrance past Candy's soft lips. Candy was generous with the sounds she made, a soft whimper ghosting across Votra's lips.

And that was all it took to completely undo her. "I want you, Candy," she breathed into Candy's mouth. She didn't care how pathetic she sounded. "I have not stopped thinking about you since this morning and I want you so, so badly."

Candy drew back and Votra immediately missed the feeling of her plush lips against hers. "Really?" Her eyes darkened with something that stirred excitement in the pit of Votra's stomach. "I guess you better take me back to your room then."

She didn't have to tell Votra twice. Votra begrudgingly peeled herself away from Candy and led her to her room. The second the door closed behind them, Candy was on her again, peppering her with feverish kisses. "Lay down," she breathed, pressing her palms flat against Votra's chest and leading her towards the bed.

Candy crawled across her slowly, torturously, pushing her to lay flat against the bed. She felt particularly un-sexy in her ratty old t-shirt and baggy pants, but Candy didn't seem to mind. Her bare knee brushed against Votra's clothed member, and she groaned at the minimal contact. "I've been thinking about you all day too," Candy murmured, skating her hands down the length of Votra's torso. "Those texts earlier were such a tease. I had to use my vibrator to get myself off, but I was imagining it was you the entire time."

Fuck. Votra reached out for Candy and was swiftly stopped as Candy captured her wrists between one hand. She pinned them above Votra's head. "Ah-ah. Not yet. I wanna tease you like you teased me earlier."

Rebellion stirred in the pit of Votra's stomach, if only because she was already so desperate. Her cock came to life behind the thin fabric of her pants. "If I recall correctly, you told me you came so hard it made you dizzy. I would hardly call that a tease."

"Mouthy girl," Candy said, grabbing Votra by the jaw with her free hand. "I made *myself* come so hard it made me dizzy. But it should have been you."

Gods, it should have been. Candy brushed her thumb across Votra's lips, and she couldn't stop herself from darting her tongue out to swirl around the pad of her thumb. Candy inhaled sharply. "Fuck, you look so good. Almost makes me wanna be nice to you."

Votra didn't want Candy to be nice to her. She wanted to be used, to be teased, to be brought to the very end of her rope only to be denied. She was almost embarrassed by how badly she wanted it.

"Please," Votra choked the word out, every nerve in her body alight with need. "Do whatever you want to me. You do not have to be nice."

Candy's lips parted with surprise. "Oh, honey, I don't think you know what you've signed yourself up for," she purred, planting a kiss to the base of Votra's throat before extricating herself from her. "Take your pants off, pretty girl."

Votra couldn't take them off fast enough. Her cock sprang to attention the second it was free from the confines of her pants, and Candy rewarded her by trailing her hand along the length of it. Her entire body thrummed with need, and she greedily pushed her hips up against nothing as Candy sat by her side watching her, taking her in.

"You're already so hard for me and I've hardly even touched you." Candy licked her lips as if preparing to devour her. Her hand found Votra again, her thumb swiping across the tip that was already leaking for her. "So beautiful. You look so good right now." She settled between Votra's legs and lowered her mouth onto her cock, and it took all of her self restraint not to shove her hips up against Candy's face.

"Candy," Votra gasped, threading her fingers in Candy's hair.

Which proved to be her first mistake. Candy pulled away, her lipstick smudged obscenely around her mouth. "I told you not to touch me yet." Votra whimpered, her wet cock even more sensitive now.

Candy rucked her skirt up around her hips, and Votra immediately wished she'd been the one to do it. She slid her longest two fingers into Votra's mouth, and she took them obediently, moaning against them as she dampened them with her desperate tongue.

"Thank you, baby." Candy dipped the same hand under the waistband of her underwear, working those same two fingers against herself. "You like watching me, don't you?"

"Yes," Votra croaked, fighting a losing battle with the desire to take herself into her fist.

But she liked relinquishing control to Candy, no matter how aggressively she liked to tease. Her cock strained with the need to come, and she fought it back the best she could.

Candy drew her hand away from herself, her breaths small and stilted. And Votra couldn't stop herself from begging, "Can I please taste you?"

And Candy was all too happy to oblige. Her fingers found Votra's mouth again, and Votra took them in greedily, the taste of Candy coating her tongue. She never wanted to forget this taste.

Candy looked upon her with heavy lidded eyes, her teeth buried in her lower lip. "Jesus fucking Christ," she whispered. "My good girl. My desperate girl. You're so fucking sexy like this."

Gods, she was *absolutely* going to come without Candy even touching her. But she didn't want to. She wanted to feel her on every inch of her skin, taste her in every corner of her mouth. She wanted Candy's control over her, even if it meant delaying her orgasm even longer.

"Tell me what you want," she whispered, leaning in to brush her nose against Votra's jaw.

"You. Fuck, I want *you*. I just want you to touch me." Votra was babbling at this point–she wasn't sure she'd ever wanted anything so badly in her life. "I want you to do whatever you want with me, but please, gods, touch me."

And then, Candy sat back and just looked at her. Her eyes moved over Votra slowly, so tenderly it made Votra's chest ache. "God, how am I supposed to tease you when you beg like that?" She skimmed her hands under Votra's shirt, easing it off her body.

Votra hadn't been fully naked in front of anyone in a long time. So much of the sex she'd had in her life had been rushed, wedged into a schedule that was typically 'too busy' for it. It was an afterthought, not something that deserved time, reverence. She could pull her dick out of her pants in an instant, and a quick fuck in the office could be slotted into their schedule when time permitted, when there weren't more important things to do.

But right now, there was nothing more important in the world than the woman hovering over Votra's rock hard member. Candy didn't take Votra into her mouth again. Instead, she pressed hot kisses everywhere but where she needed them. Her inner thighs, her lower stomach, and one teasing, painfully hot lick at the base of her cock.

"Candy, I–" Votra tried to warn her.

"Don't. Not yet. It's my turn." She smiled slyly, rising off the bed just long enough to slip her barely-there underwear down her legs and kick them off. "I wanna ride your face. Is that okay?"

Votra might actually have a heart attack. "Gods, yes." She slid down in the bed to give Candy time to straddle her, a feat that proved more difficult than expected with Votra's horns in the way. Candy nearly stumbled over them, and Votra's hands flew up to bracket her hips, keeping her steady.

This time, Candy didn't pull away from Votra's touch. Instead, she moaned against it, and it was only then that Votra could see just how aroused Candy was. Her hot, wet pussy was positioned over Votra's face, and she wasted no time in burying herself in her.

Candy gripped Votra's horns for leverage, shamelessly rutting herself into Votra's face. She couldn't breathe, and she couldn't possibly care less. The room was flooded by the litany of desperate, choked moans that Votra's movements wrested from Candy, mingling with Votra's lewd slurps.

"Shit, Votra, you're so fucking good," Candy sobbed, and Votra's breath caught as her orgasm coiled in the pit of her stomach.

She was going to come whether Candy wanted her to or not. But she didn't dare stop. She lost track of where she ended and Candy began, and she never wanted to stop feeling like that. Her fingertips dug into Candy's clothed hips and she wished more than anything that she could rip this damn dress off her.

"H-Hold on." Candy drew in a ragged breath as she moved. Votra didn't have much time to miss the feeling of Candy's arousal against her face, because all Candy did was turn around, her ass facing toward Votra now.

And then Candy took Votra into her mouth, shoving her pussy against Votra.

Votra steadied Candy's hips, lapping at her arousal as Candy took Votra into her mouth in her entirety. Her throat tightened around her tip, her moans vibrating along her length. Keeping up her movements on Candy was hard to do when she was this close to the edge.

She sunk her fingertips into Candy harder in what she hoped would come across as a warning. The last thing she wanted to do was choke Candy with her cum but the likelihood of that happening was growing stronger with each second. Her head swam as the need to come crashed over her.

But luckily, her position on Candy allowed her the ability to pull away a fraction. "Candy," she moaned. "Can I come? Please, please let me come."

Candy pulled back from Votra, her words ghosting across the tip of her cock. "Yes, baby, come for me."

And she did, harder than she had ever come in her life. Candy took in every drop of her, sliding her cum-coated tongue along the head to collect any she'd missed. And all the while, she shamelessly rutted against Votra's face, seeking out any small amount of friction that she could. Votra flattened her tongue against her and Candy cried out, the sound muffled by the cum coating her throat.

Her cum spilled across Votra's tongue, and that was nearly enough to get Votra going again. She licked Candy clean like it was her job, collecting every drop of her arousal until the stimulation became too much for Candy and she pulled away.

"Votra, holy shit," Candy laughed breathlessly, repositioning herself to straddle Votra's waist. Her plump ass settled against Votra's cock, and she willed it to behave. She leaned down, pressing her lips to Votra's. She could taste herself on Candy's lips, and weirdly, she didn't hate it. "You... you were amazing."

"Me?" Votra suddenly felt bashful, and she turned away from Candy's searing gaze. But Candy took her by the jaw and turned her face, forcing their eyes to meet again.

"I like hearing you. You're usually so quiet." Candy kissed her again and Votra laced her fingers into her hair again, selfishly holding her closer for as long as she could.

Votra took in a shuddering breath, her muscles finally relaxing from the effort of just how hard she'd come. "I will try to be louder next time."

"Next time?"

"If you want it."

Candy pulled back, smoothing her thumbs over Votra's cheekbones. "I do want it. We could go again right now, if you want." She grinned, and though every fiber of Votra's body wanted Candy again, she didn't think she had the stamina.

"Gods, do you not think you have put me through enough?" Votra teased, and Candy snorted, rolling onto her side.

"Shut up. You liked it."

She did. Too much, maybe. She was going to be thinking about this night for the rest of her life. No matter what happened, even if this was the last time... she wouldn't forget it.

Chapter Twelve

Candy

CANDY AND VOTRA DIDN'T make it to the office early the next morning. If Candy had it her way, they wouldn't have made it to the office at all. She woke up naked and tangled in Votra's long limbs and all she wanted was to stay that way.

She was surprised that Votra wasn't awake before her. She was still out cold when Candy woke up, and Candy was struck by how peaceful she looked. The seemingly ever-present creases at the corners of her lips were gone. Her face was smooth, calm. Unbothered. Candy wished she looked like this all the time.

She traced every slope of Votra's face with her fingertip; down the bony structure that almost made her look like she had a nose, across her sharp cheekbones, along her defined jaw. A pang of tenderness settled somewhere in the middle of her chest as she found herself wishing that every morning could be like this.

Could it be? Were they still just fuck buddies? Sure, last night was their first time having sex after agreeing not to, but it felt like so much more than that.

She'd let go last night, more than she'd ever let go with anyone, and she wanted to think that Votra had, too. Candy liked being domineering in the bedroom, and Ross had always hated it. He felt emasculated, relegating her to a life of always being under him, always being the one begging.

But with Votra, she lost all control but simultaneously felt more in control than she'd ever felt before. She relished the feeling of Votra coming undone under her hands. But more than that, she loved seeing the side of Votra that unabashedly demanded what she wanted. What she needed.

And Candy really liked being needed by her.

Candy let out a quiet sigh, folding her hands on top of Votra's steadily rising and falling chest and resting her chin on top of them. She'd at least let herself enjoy the peace while it lasted.

"Good morning," Votra said, her voice a low, sexy rumble that almost made Candy want to jump her bones again.

"It's not morning anymore," Candy smiled, brushing her lips across Votra's jaw. "You hungry?"

"It is not morning?" Votra's eyes flew open in a panic, and Candy pressed her palm against her chest to stop her from sitting up.

"Votra. It's fine. When's the last time you slept in this late?" she challenged, quirking her eyebrows at her. When Votra thought for a beat too long, Candy snorted. "Exactly. You obviously needed this."

Votra huffed. "We should get to the office. We have a lot to do."

"Let me take you out for lunch first." For one, she was so hungry, she felt like her stomach was caving in on itself. There was no way Votra wasn't hungry too.

But she wasn't ready for this to end. She didn't want to go back to the office and just... go back to work like she hadn't just had the best night of her life.

Votra opened her mouth to argue and Candy silenced her with her lips. "I'm taking you out and then we'll go back to work, okay?" She raked her teeth over her lower lip. "Be a good girl and say yes."

"Yes. Okay." Her answer was so quick, Candy didn't have the time to come up with another argument.

"Good. Glad we're on the same page." Candy shoved herself out of bed, belatedly realizing that the only clothes she had on hand were the skin-tight dress she'd had to recruit Votra to help wrestle her out of last night and the pair of soaked beyond reuse underwear crumpled at the end of the bed. She puffed out her cheeks, placing her hands on her hips.

"I am assuming you do not want to put on the dress from last night," Votra said, moving to sit on the edge of the bed. Her hands skimmed around Candy to rest on her stomach, and she pressed a kiss to the middle of Candy's back. She arched into it, her body already reacting more than she needed it to right now.

"Probably not." Candy moved backwards to sit in Votra's lap, pressing her ass against her already attentive cock. Votra moaned in her ear, the hands that were once on her stomach moving up to cup her breasts. Candy swiveled her hips, grinding her already wet core against Votra.

She could get used to this. Lazy, sex-soaked mornings in Votra's bed, followed by a cute little lunch date. She was learning pretty quickly that she could get Votra to bend to her will easily. She could be having cute little lunch dates *every* day.

"I thought you wanted to get lunch," Votra groaned, tweaking one of Candy's nipples between two fingers.

Candy whined at her touch, shoving her tits into Votra's hands. "Lunch can wait." Votra kissed down the length of Candy's shoulder, and Candy reached back, gripping one of Votra's horns. She didn't have hair that Candy could yank, but she kind of liked that Votra had built in handlebars.

Votra's erection was pressed against her, demanding attention, when quite easily the most unattractive sound Candy had ever heard echoed from the room next to them. "Sounds like Qaed's awake," Candy groaned.

And he was having a hell of a time, from the sounds of it. The poor guy retched so loudly, so aggressively, that every little bit of arousal in Candy shriveled up. She wrinkled her nose, falling back against Votra. "You gonna go check on him?"

"I *really* do not want to." But Votra's hands moved from Candy's boobs and she knew this was over. Fucking Qaed. "But I should. You can borrow some of my clothes if you would like to."

"Honey, nothing you own is going to fit me, I can promise you that." She peeled herself away from Votra begrudgingly. "Go check on Qaed. I'm just gonna text Xyxy and ask her to bring something over."

"Alright." Votra pulled on her pajamas from last night and headed for the door. "I apologize in advance for what you are probably going to hear. I am going to give him medicine and he is going to be *very* dramatic about it."

"You're a good sister," Candy said softly. "I'll be here when you're done."

After the most shameful Walk of Shame Candy had ever done in her life, which consisted of her wrapping herself in Votra's comforter and walking to the front door to accept a change of clothing from Xyxy, Candy was finally clothed in a pair of denim cut-offs and a black halter top. It took a while for Votra to rejoin her and, true to her word, Qaed was *incredibly* dramatic. His groans filtered through the thin walls of the apartment, and Candy didn't know how Votra had the patience for it. Sure, she'd do it for her own sister, Cori, but she'd be really annoyed about it.

When Votra came back into the bedroom, she looked positively disheveled. "I think my appetite is gone," she grunted, sloughing off her shirt in favor of yet another one of the button ups that Candy loved so much. This one was a black satin–and sleeveless–and she paired it with a blazer and pinstriped slacks that hugged her sharp hips in a way that begged for Candy to put her hands there.

So she did. She pressed a kiss to the nape of Votra's neck and was answered with a shiver. "You need to eat. We're going."

"That is easy for you to say. You did not have to see what I just saw." Votra leaned into Candy's touch, and Candy briefly considered picking up where they'd left off before Qaed so rudely interrupted them. But her stomach was growling, and she wasn't sure how much longer she could wait.

Luckily, Votra didn't make her wait very long. She flew them out to a restaurant not far from the office called Felicette, a charming little bistro that reminded Candy of the very hipster cafes that popped up on every corner in New York. Except the ones in New York didn't have cute little robot hosts with bowties.

"Hello, and welcome to Felicette!" the host chirped, a brilliant smile etched on its digital face. "How many in your party?"

"Two, please," Candy said.

The droid led them through the small dining room, across the elegant, mosaic tiled floor to a table pressed against the back wall. "Does this suit you?" it asked.

It took Candy a second to realize that Votra was looking to her for an answer. "Oh, yeah, this is great! Thank you!" Votra pulled Candy's seat out for her, at which she grinned. "Such a gentleman."

She didn't recognize anything on the menu; a small introduction on the front page told her this was food from Medras, which she was pretty sure was where Yule was from. "So, I know you're stressed that we're not at work right now, but would it help you to talk about it?" she asked, resting her chin in her palm.

Votra let out a breath like she'd been holding it. "Yes, it would. Thank you."

Poor thing. Candy wondered if she'd ever been relaxed a day in her life. "Okay, so the launch party is next week." Alright, saying that out loud *kind of* stressed her out, too. "How are you feeling about it?"

"Honestly?" Votra thanked the waiter quietly as he dropped off glasses of water for them. "I am nervous out of my mind."

"Yeah, me too," Candy said, taking a sip of water. "What are you most scared about?"

Votra went quiet, studying the menu like she was about to be tested on it. "Can I admit something silly?" Her voice was so small that it made Candy's chest constrict.

"Of course."

"I invited my parents to the launch party just before I hired you. I got a text back from one of my fathers this morning, while I was in the middle of cleaning Qaed up, telling me that they are not coming." There was a slight tremble to Votra's form as she spoke, and Candy immediately reached her hand out to take Votra's.

"Why not?" she asked softly.

"They have never approved of what I am doing. They thought that this was something I would grow out of, that I would do something worth being proud of like my other siblings." She drew in a shuddering breath, and all Candy wanted to do was pull her into her arms. "My father said that he pitied me. He checks on me because he is worried about me, because he thinks that, one day, I will stop being able to provide for myself because everything that I have worked for will fail."

"Votra," Candy whispered, squeezing her hand. She couldn't imagine how that felt. Her parents had always been her most stalwart supporters—even when Candy was sixteen and decided that her big ambition was to be a tattoo artist, her father made a vow that he would be her first client. It didn't end up happening, of course, and the world was better for it. But her parents would never tell her that.

Votra cleared her throat just in time for the server to return for their orders. Candy ordered something called braised Medran bluefish and the server respectfully dipped away and left them to their conversation.

"You're not going to fail," Candy said once the server was out of earshot.

"I know." Votra concentrated on her glass of water now. "And I think that is part of what makes this so frustrating. I wish that they wanted to celebrate with me. But they did not decline because they were busy. They just... do not want to come."

Anger that Candy didn't deserve to feel flickered in the pit of her stomach. She didn't know Votra's parents, and right now, she *really* didn't want to. But she couldn't understand how they could be anything less than proud of her.

"That's not fair." Her eyes stung with tears, and she tried her best to withhold them. Votra didn't need to comfort her. "That's why you're nervous? Because they're not gonna be there?"

"I always imagined what it would be like, to release my work into the world and look out at all of the people supporting me and see my parents standing there. I imagined they would be there, cheering the loudest, because they always did when I was little. But having that confirmation that they will not be there...." A tear rolled down Votra's cheek, and that was nearly enough to bring Candy to tears, too. "I apologize. I did not mean to get this, um, worked up about this."

"You have nothing to be sorry about," Candy said. "Thank you for telling me."

"Is your family coming?" Votra asked.

"My uncle and his husband are. My parents and my sister are still on Earth and I don't think they have any interest in traveling out here, but I know they'll be calling me on the day of the party."

She wished Votra could meet them. They'd love her—especially her dad. Her own throat grew tight, and she took a drink of water in the hopes of loosening it. "I'd love for you to meet my uncle and his husband, if you're okay with that."

"I would love to." Votra gave her a watery smile and pulled her hand away from Candy's as their server returned.

She was pretty sure her uncle Lochlan would love Votra, too. He was a pretty good judge of character. There had been many occasions where Candy had brought friends home that Lochlan immediately disliked—to an extent that was acceptable to dislike a child, of course—and Candy never understood him until inevitably, a few months down the line, said friend did something to hurt her. He was always right.

She was lost in her daydream of Votra meeting Lochlan until white-hot pain burst across the exposed skin of her thighs. Candy let out a shriek of surprise, grabbing her linen napkin from the table and immediately mopping as much sauce off her legs as she could.

"Gods, I am so sorry," the server spluttered, picking the plate up off her lap and scrambling to rescue her from the hot food.

Everything seemed to happen in a blur, but the one thing she could make out was Votra leaping from her seat. "It's okay," Candy said thickly. "I'll take care of this if you could just get me another one, please." It took every ounce of her self control to keep her voice level, to keep herself from bursting into tears.

"O-of course." The server abandoned his mission of clearing the food off her lap and scrambled away. Candy brushed the remainder of the food off her and onto the floor. The sauce left trails of irritated red skin along the length of her thighs. Damn, it had smelled so good, too.

"Come here, let me help you." Votra was already by Candy's side, hooking her arm around her to help her up. "Are you alright to walk?"

"I think so." Candy's throat was tight, her sinuses prickling with unshed tears. God, she was *really* not good with pain. "I'm so sorry."

"Stop apologizing." Votra's words were sharp but not unkind. "You did nothing wrong."

This wasn't how she wanted today to go. The morning had felt so... perfect, with the exception of Qaed's interruption. She just wanted a cute lunch date with Votra.

"Can I please take care of you?" When Votra forced Candy's gaze to meet hers, her knees immediately went weak, and it wasn't because of how much they hurt.

"...Okay."

Chapter Thirteen

Votra

A MASS OF EMOTIONS whorled in Votra as she escorted Candy into the thankfully empty restroom. Candy leaned against the counter top lined with sinks, pulling paper towels from the dispenser. Her thighs were an angry red, still plastered with sauce.

"Here, sit," Votra said, ushering her to take a seat on the counter top. She took the paper towels from Candy's hand and wet them in cold water, placing them against the irritated skin. "Are you alright?" she asked cautiously, though she knew the answer.

"Never better," Candy hissed, blowing a labored breath past her lips. "Fuck, this hurts."

Votra fought back the urge to pull Candy into her arms and instead focused her energy on plastering damp towels on Candy's thighs. The sensitive skin was beginning to bubble, which Votra had never seen before but was immediately alarmed by. "It looks bad," she said. "What can I get for you?"

"Nothing." Candy's lower lip wobbled, and she sniffled as she looked down at her poor thighs. She took in a sharp breath, dabbing at her lash line with the crook of her finger. "Sorry. I just need a second to get all this sauce off me before we go sit back down."

"It is alright, take your time," Votra said. "Are you sure you are alright?"

"Yeah." Candy's voice was weak and wholly unconvincing. She cleared her throat, pulling some of the wet towels off her leg. It didn't look much better than it had a second ago, but at least she wasn't coated in sauce anymore. She rubbed at a spot of sauce that stained the hem of her shorts, hissing through her teeth as the rough paper towel brushed against one of the young blisters forming.

And then, she burst into tears. Votra didn't stop herself from pulling Candy to her, holding her trembling form against her as she cried. Anger seared through her. Votra wasn't great in social situations by any means—if this had happened to her, she wouldn't have said a word. She honestly wouldn't have even expected her meal for free.

But seeing Candy cry made her want to cause a scene. She stroked Candy's hair gently, her other arm pulling her flush against her chest. "I will clean you up and then we will go, okay?" she murmured into Candy's sweet-smelling hair.

"No," Candy sobbed into Votra's shirt. "I know I said I wanted to leave, but I don't wanna ruin our lunch. We can stay out. I just need a second."

The anger flickering inside Votra blossomed through her chest. "Candy, you are not ruining our lunch," she said. "What happened is not your fault. You *do* know that, correct?"

"But now I'm freaking out about it and you have to stay in here with me and your food is getting cold." Candy's words came out in a flurry of tears and hiccups.

This felt like more than just misplaced guilt. Votra smoothed her hand over Candy's head. "If it makes you feel any better, my dish is meant to be eaten cold."

Candy gave a little wet laugh and pulled back from Votra, her eyes as red as her cheeks. Her dark makeup smeared around her eyes. "I'm sorry. I just don't handle pain all that well."

"You have nothing to apologize for." Votra begrudgingly untangled herself from Candy. "I am going to ask for some ointment for your legs. I will be right back."

She returned to the dining room, and their server darted to Votra's side immediately. "Is she alright? I'm so sorry, I didn't mean to—"

"Do you have any burn ointment?" Votra asked, her tone clipped.

"Yes, of course!" He scurried away and returned with it in record speed, thrusting a giant handful of silver sachets into Votra's hands. "We have some more food coming out for her as well."

Suddenly, the last thing Votra wanted was to be in this restaurant anymore. "Please pack it up to go," she said in as level of a tone as she could manage.

"I understand. I'm so, so sorry, I really am," he said, bowing his head profusely before leaving her again.

Candy had stopped crying by the time Votra returned. She didn't speak, settling with just leaning into Votra as she applied the ointment to Candy's legs. This was not an appropriate time to ogle them, Votra told herself.

"That feels a lot better," Candy murmured, pulling away from Votra to admire her handiwork. "Wow, my legs look like shit."

"They kind of do," Votra joked. Candy giggled, which only made Votra feel marginally better about this whole thing. "Are you alright?"

"Yeah. I'm really sorry that I kind of freaked out just now." Candy leaned back against the mirror behind her. "And thank you for being so patient with all of that." Candy's eyes watered again and she sniffled, rubbing at them with the heels of her palms. "God, I'm sorry. I'm being so dumb right now."

Votra's heart bottomed out into her stomach. "Why are you doing that?"

"Doing what?"

"Belittling the way you feel. You just had food spilled on you that was so hot, you have actual burns." Votra folded her arms over her chest. "You know that you are allowed to have feelings, right?"

Candy's lips trembled, and she dipped her head to stare into her lap. "Oh, trust me, I *do* have feelings. And they're always really big and then I cry and I make it everyone else's problem."

"Who told you that?" There was a protective edge to her voice that she tried to tuck away, but to no avail.

"My ex." Candy laughed humorlessly. "I've always been like this. I never just feel a little bummed or a little excited or a little scared. Everything feels *huge* and Ross hated that. The first time I got to see him shoot a scene for a movie, I cried like a baby. I was so proud of him. And he... pretended like he didn't know me. He told his coworkers that he didn't know how I got on set."

Votra felt like she couldn't draw in a deep enough breath. Ross should consider himself lucky he didn't live in Kratos, because he would be in for a hell of a time if he did.

"Perhaps this is rude to ask... but why did you stay with him?"

Candy nibbled her lower lip. "Y'know, everyone asked me the same thing. I dunno... I guess I hoped he would change. I always wanna assume the best in people, even if they show me over and over again that they suck." She sniffed. "I was trying so hard to make him likeable in my head that I let him make me think I was the unlikeable one."

"I hope you understand now how untrue that is," Votra said quietly, brushing a smudge of eyeliner from Candy's cheek. "You are the most genuine person I have ever met. I wish that I could be like you."

Candy pulled Votra in by her forearms, letting her stand between her legs. "I like you the way you are, though. I like the Votra that goes on tangents about things she loves. And the Votra that's open about how she feels. You're a really genuine person, too, when you let yourself be."

Votra froze under Candy's touch. She tried not to let herself hone in on the fact that Candy thought she went off on *tangents*. She knew she talked too much. She thought she'd mastered the art of speaking just enough, not enough to take up too much space but enough to be likeable. Enough that she wouldn't be branded as antisocial, but not so much that she was considered self-absorbed.

Maybe she hadn't quite mastered it yet.

"I'm saying that I like you, Votra. Don't overthink it." She placed a hand on Votra's shoulder to support herself as she slid off the counter top, wincing as she did. "Okay. I can do this. Should we go eat?"

Wait, what? Votra blinked at Candy, still processing exactly what had happened. "Oh, um, I told them to pack it up to go. I thought you might want to sit somewhere more comfortable," she stammered.

Candy *liked* her? Maybe she was imagining that. Maybe there was no meaning behind her words beyond the fact that she didn't mind hearing Votra infodump.

"You read my mind," Candy grinned, looping her arm around Votra's.

Before they left the bathroom, Votra stopped her. "You have so much makeup all over your face," she laughed, brushing her thumb across a smudge of eyeliner on Candy's cheek. "There you go."

"Thanks." Candy paused. "For everything."

Votra drew in a deep breath. "I understand what you are going through. I... also dated someone who was a bit of a closed door. She was not as controlling as Ross, but she *did* think that emotions only complicated things. And I am still learning how untrue that is."

Candy's eyes on Votra went soft. "We can unlearn it together," she said. She rose on her tiptoes and pressed a feather light kiss to Votra's cheek. "Come on. I'm hungry."

They returned to their table just as the server was delivering two boxes of food. "Your check has been taken care of," he said, more to Votra than to Candy. *That was rude.* Votra opened her mouth to say exactly that, but Candy cut her off.

"Thank you so much!" she said, collecting their food into her hands. "We appreciate that a lot." Votra still wasn't exactly won over, but something told her Candy wouldn't want any more attention on her.

"We are so sorry, again," the server said, his eyes on Votra again, and Votra didn't keep quiet this time.

"Could you please apologize to my...." Her what? Colleague? *Employee?* Her brain tossed the word *partner* into the mix before immediately throwing it out.

But the server didn't think much of it. "Of course. I am so sorry, miss," he said, directly to Candy this time. "I hope that you will give us another try one day."

We will not, Votra wanted to say, but Candy interjected. "We will! Thank you!" Votra ushered her out of the restaurant before she could make friends with the server that had gotten them into this situation in the first place.

"Aww. Poor guy. I hope he doesn't get in trouble," Candy said as they stepped into the cool afternoon air. Votra felt quite the opposite.

Chapter Fourteen

Candy

ONCE THEY WERE OUTSIDE the restaurant, all previous discomfort had flown completely out the window.

"It's so cute out here," she said, reaching her hand out and splaying her fingers. It felt like a late summer day in New York, minus the ever-present piss smell and streets littered with trash. Veterok-III's atmosphere closely resembled Earth's, but the air was crisper, cleaner. Warmer. The courtyard was pristinely clean, dotted with droids picking up whatever trash they happened upon. Never in Candy's life did she think she'd be happy to see astroturf, but right now, all she wanted to do was roll around in it.

They fell into step beside each other, Candy having to take slightly longer strides to keep up with Votra. Droids in the shape of birds flitted around them, letting out mechanical chirps that absolutely delighted Candy.

The stretch of concrete pathway that led away from the restaurant opened up to a swath of astroturf cut away from the concrete. Above it in the air was a screen, a movie Candy didn't recognize playing across it. The sound from it was quiet, subtitles in Universal rolling across the bottom of the screen.

"You are never going to believe this," Votra said, eyes glued to the screen. "This is *Outlaw Koran.*"

Excitement bubbled in Candy's chest. "Let's watch it!" She pulled her arm from Votra's and bounded onto the green, spreading her arms and letting the warm sun kiss her skin. The homesickness got easier over time, but this was the happiest she'd been in a while.

Votra caught up to her, sloughing the jacket from her arms. And honestly, Candy couldn't bring herself to pretend not to stare. Candy was no stranger to Votra's bare arms by now, but it wasn't often that she got to see them in broad daylight. Votra's top didn't reveal her chest like most of her shirts did, but it did put on display long, prominent veins that branched up the length of her arms. Candy wanted to trail her fingers along them. Or her tongue.

"Is this alright?" Votra asked, stopping at a spot far enough from the other filmgoers to give them some privacy but not so far that the screen was hard to see.

"Perfect," Candy said. Votra passed the food containers to Candy and laid her jacket across the prickly plastic grass.

"Here, sit on this. I am sure this type of terrain will be uncomfortable against your legs."

Candy's heart sped up as she sat. This felt so... romantic. She immediately pushed the thought away and sat. Votra was right–the jacket was much better on her legs than the grass would have been. "Thank you," she said sweetly. Votra settled next to her, her arm lightly brushing against Candy's.

Eating was the last thing on her mind as Votra handed her food over. The bluefish smelled incredible. Candy allowed herself to lean on Votra a little as she adjusted herself carefully so as not to let her thighs touch.

Votra's eyes were trained on the screen in front of them, reflections of the movie dancing across her dark irises. She wondered what little Votra had been like, sitting on the floor of her living room, excitement dancing in her eyes as she watched this movie–to Candy's delight, Koran was just as hot as she imagined her.

Votra watched Candy as she took her first bite of bluefish. "What do you think?" she asked, gesturing to it with a nod of her head.

Candy took a careful bite, still a little afraid of it after what it had done to her legs, and warm spices exploded across her tongue. It almost reminded her of Indian food from back home–creamy, spicy, rich. Some sort of pearled grain sat beneath the soupy chunks of... vegetable?

Whatever it was, she was in love with it. "That's fucking amazing, oh my God."

"I am glad you like it. I was a bit concerned at first–the flavor profiles of Medran food are quite different than Earth food, so I was not sure how much you would like it."

Candy's eyebrows crept up. "What do you know about Earth food?"

"I know that there are many different types. Among the planets out here, the food is generally quite uniform–Medran food is typically briny, medicinal, healthy.

Daocurian food is always spicy. And food from Alqen is entirely vegetable based, with a lot of bitter elements. But on Earth, you have so many different kinds of flavors.

"And then *cake*. Cake is the thing that I want to try the most. So many of the Earth novels I have read mention cake and always make it sound so good. It is a celebration dish, correct?"

God, Votra was cute. "Sometimes." Candy's food was forgotten in her lap in favor of just… listening. She could listen to Votra talk all day. "Not all Earth food is sweet, y'know."

"I know. I would especially like to try Indian cuisine one day. It sounds the most like the food we have on Alqen–very vegetable-based, with a few staple sauces that we use on most dishes." Votra shoved a bite of food into her mouth, and Candy already missed her voice.

"Maybe I'll take you to try it one day," Candy said. "And then we can have cake afterwards."

"That sounds like a plan." Votra returned her attention to the screen just as Koran and Calypso shared an intense, passionate kiss. Damn, maybe she *did* want to watch this movie. "What is living on Earth like?"

Candy mulled over the question, popping a forkful of food into her mouth. "Earth is honestly pretty different, depending on what part you grew up on. My part of Earth is pretty wealthy, in the grand scheme of things. If you don't consider all the debt." She snorted. "I grew up in a big city. My dad stayed at home with me and my sister when she was born, and my mom worked. A lot. But she was always around when she could be.

"And then there's my Uncle Lochlan. He was around just as much as my parents were. I think it pisses my mom off, how alike we are." She pushed a piece of fish around in its container, fighting back the homesickness rising in her chest. "I'm really lucky. I've always been surrounded by love, and my parents worked hard to get to where they were. My uncle put my mom through college, and I know he worked his ass off to do it. And thanks to what he did, my mom was able to put me through college, too." Her attempts to hold back her tears proved futile, and she brushed them away as they fell. "Sorry. You weren't even asking about them. Earth is my home, but when I think about Earth, they're what I think about."

"It must be nice, growing up so surrounded by love," Votra said. Half of her food was gone already. "Your family sounds wonderful."

"They are," Candy said. "Do you have any other siblings, or is it just Qaed?"

"I have another sibling. Vendi. He is three years younger than me and he could not be less like me." Her gaze on the screen was unfocused, but less stony at the mention of Vendi. "He is a force of nature, to say the very least. Perhaps you would like him. He is a bounty hunter."

"Oh, a bounty hunter *and* he looks like you? Can you give me his comm info?" Candy teased, and Votra nudged her with her shoulder.

"She reminds me a lot of you."

Candy cringed. That wasn't a good thing. She didn't want to remind Votra of her *sibling,* of all people. "In what way?" she asked, almost afraid of the answer.

"She is extremely hard headed," Votra said, earning a playful smack from Candy. "She has been through a lot in her life. But somehow, she believes in the good of all people, just like you. I wish I had inherited that trait from her."

"I think it's just because I was raised by people who never gave me a reason to think people could be bad," Candy said. "People are good, Votra. Maybe not all of them, but a lot of them. You just have to believe in the ones that prove their goodness to you."

Something Candy couldn't place flashed across Votra's face. "I have spent a lot of my life around people who have given me no reason to believe in inherent good," she said quietly. She turned to face Candy, her eyes curving into crescents as she smiled. "But I suppose I have met some recently that might change my mind."

All Candy wanted to do was kiss her. But for some reason, she felt like she shouldn't.

This had been so easy up until now. Working, with the occasional break for sex. For all Candy knew, she'd passed the threshold of contract-breaking sex and they were about to go back to a life of all work, no play.

"Um, I think I'm gonna throw the rest of this away. Are you done?" Candy asked, rising from her spot on the grass. Shit, that hurt.

Votra blinked up at her. "Oh, yes. I am. Thank you," she said, passing her container to Candy.

When she returned to Votra, Votra was standing, dusting off her legs. "I guess we should get back to work, huh?" Candy said.

"Yes, I think we should." Votra went to retrieve her jacket from the ground, but Candy dove for it at the same time. Their hands brushed, sending a jolt through Candy's body.

God, she was fucked. Her gaze froze on Votra for a moment, but Votra was the first to pull away. She allowed Candy to pick up the jacket, taking it from her when she offered it. "Sorry. I hope it's not too dirty."

Votra smiled, folding it into the crook of her arm. "It is fine," she said, squinting her eyes against the artificial sun. Sometimes, Votra looked so... cat-like. It was way cuter than it needed to be. "Are you certain you can work like this? You must be in pain."

The throbbing pain in her thighs had taken a backseat to the swirl of much more pressing feelings coursing through her. Like the fact that she was weirdly turned on right now.

"Nah, I'm good," Candy said with a dismissive flick of her wrist. "Let's go."

They crossed the field and returned to the pavement, Candy struggling to keep up with Votra. "Your legs are long. You have to slow down," she said, hooking her hand around Votra's forearm to force her into the same pace.

Votra laughed, her steps slowing. "Of course, my apologies," she said. Damn Votra and her charming, gentlemanly way of talking. It never failed to make Candy's stomach feel like a pool of goo.

They returned to the restaurant's shuttle bay, much emptier now that lunch time was over. Votra's shuttle was one of only a handful in the entire bay. Candy supposed she should feel guilty that they'd wasted so much of their day out, but she couldn't bring herself to.

"I had a good time," Candy said after a beat of silence. "I know I said it already but... thank you for–"

Votra silenced her with her lips, and the kiss was softer than any of their kisses before, as if Votra was afraid she was going to break her. Candy felt as if she might melt into a puddle if Votra didn't hold her.

As if reading her mind, Votra's arms slid around Candy's waist and pulled her close. And Candy let her.

Chapter Fifteen

Votra

VOTRA'S MOUTH FOUND CANDY'S the second they were out of the shuttle at the office. They disconnected long enough to get into the office, but the second the door closed behind them, Candy sunk into Votra again. "Where should we go?" Votra asked between kisses.

Candy trailed her fingers over the collar of Votra's shirt. "Can we... go into the virtual reality room?"

Votra's cock immediately twitched with interest. She was no stranger to the fact that the virtual reality part of Starcrossed would be used to curate backdrops for sex, but she'd never considered trying it herself. And suddenly, it was all she wanted.

"Absolutely." She took Candy by the hand and all but dragged her into the virtual reality room. Candy was on her the second the door closed behind them, trailing hot, needy kisses down the slope of Votra's neck. She tapped her comm with trembling fingers, and the room immediately morphed around them. A fireplace crackled in one corner of the room, the steel floor below them replaced by pock-marked hardwood. The bed was no longer supported by a steel frame; it was now a comically small four-poster bed with maroon curtains that tumbled down from each poster. Votra knew she was imagining it, but it almost felt warmer than it had before.

"Wow, how romantic," Candy breathed against Votra's collarbone. Her mouth moved up to her jaw, nipping at the sensitive skin. "Come fuck me on this fancy bed."

She didn't even make it onto the bed fully before Candy was in her lap. She winced a little as she rested her legs on either side of Votra's. "Are you–"

"I'm fine," Candy said shortly. "I just need you so bad right now I can't fucking stand it."

Votra nearly choked. Candy wasn't lying; Votra could feel how wet she was through the fabric of her slacks. Her large fingers fumbled with the button of Candy's shorts and Candy rose off her for just long enough to slide them and her undwear off and kick them to the floor.

She wasted no time in grinding her hips against the ridged plate atop Votra's leg. "Fuck, you feel so good," she breathed.

But Votra was greedy. She didn't want Candy to come just from riding her leg. "Stop," she murmured, voice thick and husky with want. "Let me take care of you."

Candy whimpered at Votra's words. "Touch me then," she demanded, resting her hands on either side of Votra's neck.

Votra didn't have to be told twice. She slipped her hand between Candy's legs, reveling in the feeling of her soaking wet pussy against her fingers. Candy rode her hand, a series of sharp, desperate moans spilling past her lips.

"What do you want, darling?" Votra asked breathily. The word slipped out of her, unbidden, drawn out by the feeling of affection for Candy that tightened her chest.

Gods, she was getting into dangerous territory. Every time she and Candy slept together, she felt herself growing closer and closer to that line between sexual attraction and actual affection.

Or maybe that line was far behind her. Her need to make Candy come was created by so much more than a need to also get herself off. After the day she'd had, all Votra wanted to do was make Candy feel *good*. To lessen some of her pain, at least a little bit.

"Remember when you said you wanted me on top of you? So you could watch me take you?" Candy fumbled with Votra's zipper, and Votra immediately groaned at the contact. "That's what I want. I wanna be full of you."

At this rate, Votra was going to come before Candy got any closer to her. A pathetic "please" was all she could manage.

She'd be lying if she said she hadn't tucked herself into bed on a few of her loneliest nights with the thought of this exact thing happening. Candy guided her cock out of her underwear and brushed her thumb across the slit, which was already leaking precum. The heat in the pit of her stomach flickered into a needy, all-consuming flame, and she desperately clung to her arousal as Candy positioned her against her entrance.

She lowered herself onto Votra slowly, sinking her nails into Votra's shoulders for leverage. Votra took in a shuddering breath as she willed herself not to push herself into Candy.

Gods, Candy looked beautiful like this. Her head rolled back, eyes heavily lidded as she lowered herself onto Votra still, slowly, teasingly, until she was buried to the hilt. The flames of the fireplace flickered across her pale features, and Votra wished she could burn the image into her mind forever.

"Move. Please," Candy groaned, and Votra was more than happy to oblige. Her hands bracketed Candy's soft hips as they angled around her, Votra pressing herself against Candy as much as she could.

Votra was pretty sure she could stay like this forever and never grow tired of it. Candy's heat around her was addictive; her walls tight, throbbing, welcoming around her. She reached a hand down between Candy's legs, one thick finger circling Candy's clit.

"Oh, *fuck,*" Candy immediately cried out, her hips jerking towards Votra's hand now. She let out a string of curses, her fingernails digging harder now into the flesh of Votra's shoulders. "Don't stop, please, don't stop."

Votra wasn't sure there was anything in this galaxy that could make her. She peppered kisses along Candy's jaw, down her neck, across her clothed shoulder, everywhere she could reach. She was dangerously close herself, but she wouldn't dare let herself come until Candy had.

Candy wasn't making that easy for her, though. "You're fucking me so good," she panted. "God, you feel amazing. Your cock is perfect." Every word went directly between Votra's legs and every muscle in her body clenched.

"I want to feel you come around me," Votra breathed against the hot skin of Candy's neck.

Candy clenched around Votra, her walls choking Votra's cock as she called out her name, the word lost in a tumble of moans. Votra barely managed to pull herself out in time to come as well, ribbons of light blue cum streaking Candy's shirt.

Candy giggled breathlessly, unbuttoning her blouse and tossing it onto the floor. "You are so good to me," she breathed, and trailed her tongue along Votra's jawline.

"I'll forgive you for finishing all over my shirt. I don't have another one here, though, so...."

"I do. You can borrow one of mine."

Candy jutted her lower lip out. "Or... I could just not wear one...."

Wouldn't she get cold? Votra narrowed her eyes, trying to pick up exactly what Candy was putting out, and Candy finally rolled her eyes. "What, you want me to put my tits away?" But she smiled, resting her hands on either side of Votra's face. "I'm trying to flirt with you."

Oh. *Oh.*

"I, um, you could... not wear a shirt... if you want. If you will not be uncomfortable."

"Stop being so considerate and think with your dick for once." Candy moved off Votra's lap and Votra immediately missed her warmth.

Candy tugged her top off and tossed it to the floor with her shorts, and every little bit of moisture immediately evaporated from Votra's mouth. Candy leaned down in front of Votra, resting her hands on either of the chair's arm rests. "You were so good to me today," she purred, and Votra's cock immediately started to come back to life. "Your whole swooping in and rescuing me, taking care of me... holding me when I needed you." Her voice softened a fraction, and she tilted Votra's chin up with a single manicured finger. "I wanted to thank you properly. Can I?"

Votra drew in a shuddering breath. She wished she could take a picture of Candy, looking the way that she looked right now, in nothing but lingerie and heels. "Please," Votra choked out.

Candy knelt between Votra's legs, a smile playing at her lips. "You're already hard again? Is it because I'm telling you how good you are?" She dipped her head down, brushing her lips across Votra's thickening cock. Votra's breathing was growing labored, demanding–she didn't want to be as fast this time as she was before, but gods, Candy did something to her.

She trailed her hands along Votra's length, admiring it, worshipping it. She trailed kisses along the shaft then took the head into her mouth.

Votra's hand instinctively came down to clasp in Candy's hair. "Fuck, your mouth feels so good," she panted, and she swore she could feel Candy smile against her. Candy swirled her tongue around the head, across the slit. A litany of moans filled the space around them, and Candy moaned against Votra. The vibration sent a thrill through Votra's body.

"Candy, please," Votra begged. She didn't even know what she was begging for. All she knew was that her vision was swimming with pleasure.

Candy's small hand circled Votra's member, pumping it slowly while she continued teasing the tip with her mouth. Votra couldn't stop herself from moving her hips against Candy's kiss-swollen mouth.

Votra had never been like this before. Just like with every other aspect of her life, she generally liked control in the bedroom. But she found herself wanting to submit to Candy, to let herself be putty in her hands. And fuck, did it feel good to beg for her.

"Talk to me, baby," Candy commanded, the vibrations of her voice reverberating down Votra's length.

There was no shortage of words Votra wanted to say to her. "Gods, I love when you suck my dick. I love seeing you on your knees for me. I love how pretty you look with my cock in your mouth. I love–"

I love you. The words were so dangerously close to slipping out, and Votra stifled them with a not entirely faked moan.

Maybe it was just the adrenaline talking. Just the euphoria of spending the last twenty-four hours with her, of having more mind-blowing sex than she'd had in the last five years of her life.

The words clung to her tongue, and she was almost afraid to speak again for fear of them slipping out. Or maybe this would be a good time. Candy couldn't reply with a cock in her mouth.

She took Votra deeper into her mouth, and Votra cried out, her grip on Candy's hair tightening. Her stomach clenched a little as the fleeting wonder of how many people Candy had done this to crossed her mind. How many other people had been lucky enough to be in Candy's beautiful, expert mouth? Greedily, she wished she'd been the only one.

Candy pulled back, quickening the pace of her hand on Votra. "Let me taste you," she whispered before taking Votra back into her mouth. That was all Votra needed to shatter in Candy's hands. She filled Candy's mouth with her cum, a rivulet trickling out of the corner of her lips. She looked up at Votra through thick lashes, and the sight was enough to stir her cock again.

Votra leaned down to brush her thumb across Candy's lips, and Candy's tongue darted out to slide along the length of her thumb, collecting the stray bead of cum that Votra had wiped from her skin.

Gods, this woman was magnificent.

She couldn't let herself get riled up again. She gestured with a finger for Candy to rise from the floor, and Candy moved onto her lap, her back pressed against Votra's chest. Her beautiful, plump ass came to rest right on Votra's spent cock–or what she *thought* was spent. It threatened to come to life again under Candy, and surely, Candy could feel it too.

The grinding of Candy's ass against her only confirmed that. Votra groaned, sliding her hands around Candy's front to cup her breasts. "You are insatiable," Votra groaned, sinking her teeth into the sweet-smelling skin of Candy's shoulder.

"Do you want a break?" Candy asked genuinely, her movements against Votra stilling.

"No," Votra said a little too quickly. Candy giggled.

"Good. Don't plan on getting any work done any time soon."

Chapter Sixteen

Candy

CANDY STAYED AT THE office for entirely too long once they finally got back to work; they had a lot of catching up to do after the distraction that was their lunch date and the multiple orgasms each of them had afterwards. The gravity of the looming launch party had finally settled in on them, and they managed to crank out a few hours' worth of work before Candy's eyes stung so badly, she could hardly keep them open anymore.

But she wanted to stay at the office until Votra left, and she was going to do it. Even if she felt like her eyeballs were going to fall out of her skull.

"You doing okay over there?" she asked, silently hoping Votra would say no.

She didn't know why she expected that. "Yes. Are you?"

"How are your eyes even open right now? I feel like this screen is burning through my retinas." She squeezed her eyes shut and immediately, it was like someone was driving thousands of tiny needles into them.

"You do not have to stay," Votra said, not unkindly. "My eyes are more suited for this than yours. You should take a break. Go home and get some rest."

Candy really wanted to argue, but she couldn't bring herself to. She hadn't realized that it was nearly midnight until she looked down at her comm.

She pushed herself back from her chair and stood, hovering for a second. Even after letting Votra fuck her senseless eight hours ago, they'd fallen back into their quiet rhythm, and everything still felt weirdly normal.

Maybe she was wrong to expect something to change between them. Not everyone was like Candy, after all. She'd tried the whole casual thing a few times before, and it had only ever landed her in relationships. That was how she'd ended up with Ross. She couldn't sleep with someone without getting too attached. And God, was she attached to Votra.

Now she understood why Votra didn't want them doing this. The lines of professionalism were well and truly blurred by this point. Was Votra telling her to go home as her boss, or as someone who cared about her?

"Okay," she said, hands on the back of her chair. "Are you gonna head out soon?"

"Probably. I am quite tired." Votra pushed away from her desk, turning in her chair to look at Candy. "Let me know when you get home."

That was new. Bosses didn't say that to their employees. "You too." She slipped her jacket from the back of her chair. Would it be weird to give Votra a goodnight kiss?

Votra turned back towards her computer, and Candy took that as her sign to go. A goodnight kiss would *definitely* be weird.

It was well after midnight when Candy got home, and unsurprisingly, Xyxy was still awake. She was draped across Yule's lap, a rerun of Dr. Love's Biology playing on the television. They looked cozy, both of them in their pajamas. "Damn, girl, is Votra paying you for all that overtime?" Xyxy asked.

Candy immediately felt her cheeks flush. "Shut up." Xyxy's eyebrows shot up, but luckily, she didn't really question it. "We went out for lunch and got a little... distracted, so I stayed late."

"Votra got distracted in the middle of her workday?" It was Yule's turn to be surprised. "That's the least Votra thing I've ever heard."

"Yeah, well, I can be pretty distracting." She couldn't help the salacious grin that spread across her cheeks, and she plopped onto the sofa next to Yule with a hiss. The throbbing in her thighs had dulled a lot since lunch, but the pressure of her tight shorts against the still sensitive skin didn't feel great.

"Oh my gods. Did you two fuck?" Xyxy shot straight up in her seat.

Well, they did. But that wasn't why Candy was sore. She pursed her lips. "Maaaaybe."

Xyxy let out an ear-splitting squeal. "I knew it! I literally told Yule I would have put money on you two fucking again."

Yule rolled all three of her eyes before they settled on Candy's legs. "That doesn't look like a sex injury, though. What happened to you?"

Candy grimaced. "We went out for lunch and the waiter spilled my food on me. It's not as bad as it looks."

"Gods, are you okay?" Yule said immediately, all but shoving Xyxy off her. "I've got some stuff to fix you up with. You can take your shorts off if you want. I promise I won't be weird about it."

She didn't have to tell Candy twice. She peeled her shorts from her legs carefully and tossed them to the floor.

Yule scurried into her bedroom, leaving Xyxy to immediately wrap her arms around Candy from the side. "Y'know, I've been rooting for you and Votra ever since you met at my party. You're welcome for that, by the way."

The party simultaneously felt like ages ago and just yesterday. In the grand scheme of things, she still hadn't known Votra for all that long. But she also kind of felt like she'd known Votra her entire life. And as much as she didn't want to admit it, it *was* all thanks to Xyxy. "I would've met Votra through work anyway, y'know."

Candy's dad had always been a believer in fate—his go to saying was 'What is meant to be, will be,' and Candy had always lived by it. Sometimes, she didn't entirely understand it. There was no way that being with Ross for five years was meant to happen, but at the same time, the breakup was what brought her to the Kratos galaxy in the first place.

The breakup was what led her to Votra, and she couldn't help but hope that their meeting was fate, too.

"Move," Yule said as she returned to the living room, shooing Xyxy away as she knelt on the floor between Candy's legs. "I still can't believe you and Votra slept together."

Admitting it to Yule made her a lot more bashful than admitting it to Xyxy. "Yeah, we did. We have, uh...." What *did* they have? Did they have a friends with benefits agreement? After all, Votra had called it quits on their contract. Their relationship was fully up for negotiation.

Yule rifled through the metal box sitting in her lap. "I'm just kind of surprised to hear that about Votra. She's always been a bit of a lover girl."

Votra? *Her* Votra? No—not her Votra. "Really?"

"Yeah. But I think her breakup with Zeele changed things a lot." Yule ripped open a sachet of some sort of gel and squeezed it onto one of Candy's legs. She hissed against the cold, but it felt incredible on her inflamed skin.

Zeele. Votra had never mentioned her name, and Candy hated that it was pretty. Something settled in the pit of her stomach that she didn't like.

Jealousy? Candy wasn't a jealous person, and she *especially* didn't like holding herself up against other women.

"What happened between Votra and Zeele anyway?" Candy asked. She wasn't sure she really *wanted* to know, but she couldn't ignore the curiosity nagging at her.

Yule's hands were cool on Candy's thighs; the ointment didn't soak into her slippery skin, letting it sit like a cold blanket atop Candy's irritated legs. "Votra never really talked about the specifics. But I do know that she stole a lot of Votra's work when they broke up and made another dating app."

"Yeah, a shittier one. You can't type more than three hundred characters in a message without paying ten credits a month," Xyxy frowned. "LoveNet is ass and everyone knows it."

Irritation simmered in the pit of Candy's stomach. "Wait, she *stole* Votra's work?"

"Pretty sure. LoveNet literally came out a week after they broke up. There's no way she didn't steal it," Yule said, rising from her spot on the floor. She passed Candy a few packets of the ointment she'd put on her. "Put a thick layer of this on every day until it heals up."

"Thanks," Candy said numbly. She could feel her friends' eyes boring into her, and she sighed, leaning her head back into the couch cushions.

Xyxy rested her head against Candy's shoulder. "You should tell her how you feel, you know."

"Yeah. Votra is *really* bad at picking up hints. Like, laughably so," Yule piped in. "You're going to have to spell it out word for word for her."

The thought of that was terrifying. Emotional vulnerability hadn't exactly served her well in relationships before. Votra may have said that she liked how genuine Candy was, but she wasn't sure she'd appreciate that genuineness when it came in the form of a confession of love.

Love? Did she... *love* Votra?

"Yeah, and lose my job?" Candy snorted.

"She's not gonna fire you. She needs you," Xyxy pointed out. "I mean, the launch event is literally in two weeks. She'd be totally fucked without you."

She knew Xyxy was just trying to make her feel better, but the inkling that Votra was only keeping her around for that reason wedged somewhere in the center of her chest and made it hard to breathe. "I'm gonna go to bed and probably spiral about this until I fall asleep," she said, standing and giving Yule a hug. "Thanks for fixing up my legs. They feel a lot better already."

She retreated to her room before either of her roommates could press her more about Votra. Because honestly, she didn't even know what she would say.

She wanted to tell Votra how she felt. God, did she wanna just get it off her chest. But the thought of what could come afterwards terrified her.

Maybe this was something better kept to herself. What Votra didn't know couldn't hurt her.

A message from Votra buzzed from her comm.

> Are you home?

> yea!! sorry, im so sleepy i totally forgot to message you

> are you home too?

> Yes, just arrived.

There was a beat of silence before her next message.

> Goodnight, Candy. I am sorry today was not an easy day for you.

Oh, today had been far from difficult. Whatever magical healing ointment Yule had put on her was working wonders—the throbbing in her thighs had dulled to an annoying ache. If anything, Votra was the cause of the more prominent pain, throbbing between her legs. But it was a pain she could easily get used to.

> you made it a lot better. thank you again seriously. i dont know what i wouldve done without you

> goodnight votra <3

Chapter Seventeen

Votra

THE APARTMENT SHOULD HAVE been quiet when Votra woke up the next morning. Qaed hadn't come home last night, which meant that she'd get to have a meditative morning before getting ready for work.

Except for the fact that someone decided to bang on her door with all of their might, startling Votra so badly while she was brushing her teeth that she stabbed herself in the gums with the head of her toothbrush.

She all but threw her toothbrush on the counter, immediately irritated. If that was Qaed, she was actually going to kill him.

"Hold on," she called, padding from her bathroom to the living room. "Did you forget your key again?"

"Since when do I have a key?" The voice that answered her was definitely not Qaed's. Votra opened the door, only to be greeted by the sheepish grin of her much larger younger sibling.

With a bandaged arm and—was that blood on his face? Votra cursed under her breath. It wasn't hard to venture a guess as to what happened to Vendi, but that didn't make Votra stress any less.

"Did you come straight over after a job?" Votra said, clicking her tongue disapprovingly. She brushed her thumb over the bloodstain on Vendi's cheek, trying not to wonder too much whose blood it was. "Come inside. You are a mess."

"Not *straight* over," Vendi said, raising a hand in surrender. "I had to wrap this up first."

Which meant that Votra was going to finish the job. She supposed she should be honored that her little sibling was so excited to see her that he would forgo proper medical treatment. But Votra wasn't a medic, and Vendi was going to well and truly destroy his body if they kept going like this.

Vendi followed Votra into the apartment, unceremoniously flopping onto the couch. "You had better not get any blood on my white sofa," Votra called as she disappeared into her room for her first aid kit.

"I will not! I am not bleeding anymore!" Vendi called back. "I think!"

Votra groaned, bringing the first aid kit back into the living room. "If you are, I will make you clean it up." Her threat was empty—she wouldn't let Vendi lift a finger while she was here.

She sat on the couch next to Vendi, gingerly taking her arm into her hands. "What happened this time?" she asked, carefully removing the crudely wrapped bandage from Vendi's arm. "This looks horrible, Vendi."

"Oh, it is not that bad," Vendi said dismissively, hardly flinching as Votra removed the bandage pressed directly against the wound. "Caught the edge of a phaser beam. Barely nicked me."

Votra would beg to disagree. The skin of Vendi's outer forearm was singed, a chunk of tissue actually missing. From Votra's experience with patching up both Qaed and Vendi, phaser beam wounds were typically clean, aside from the charred skin. The beams were hot enough to stop infection in its tracks, but the healing process was certainly not going to be comfortable.

"Barely nicked me," Votra repeated in a gruff, mocking tone. "You are unbelievable."

Over the years, Yule had stocked Votra up with healing ointments and salves from Medras, which worked wonders on phaser beam wounds. Votra just wished she didn't have to use them so much.

"Oh, come on. You have *definitely* seen worse," Vendi said, wincing at the cool gel on his arm. She had, but that didn't mean she wanted to keep on seeing it.

"You really should have gotten this professionally looked at," Votra said. "This is going to scar."

"You think I am not used to scars?" Every time Vendi came home, his body bore at least one or two new scars, and even if Vendi was used to it, Votra certainly wasn't. She didn't like the constant reminders of the danger Vendi spent his every day in.

"Just because you are used to them does not mean you should continue to let it happen."

"Maybe one day, someone will find them attractive." Vendi tried to grin, but she immediately winced as Votra sprayed an antiseptic on the wound.

Votra rolled her eyes. "Are you staying at home for a while?"

"Probably." His eyes settled on Votra, and this time, it was her turn to squirm. "When was the last time you went back?"

Votra knew exactly where this was going. Vendi had always been closer to their parents than Votra had, and they always had a roundabout way of asking about Votra without talking to her directly. "It has been a while," she said shortly, wrapping a bandage around Vendi's thick arm. "Have you seen them since you have been back?"

"Not yet. But I will probably go see them next. I told them I was coming back into the galaxy and they–" She paused. "I am sorry. I did not come here to nag you about our parents."

It certainly felt like she did. But Votra kept her mouth shut. Visits with Vendi had become so infrequent since she became a bounty hunter. If she wasn't traipsing the galaxy, tracking down her mark, she was on Alqen, receiving praise enough for two siblings.

"What have you been doing? How is... the app? Are you still working on that?"

How is your little project going? Is it worth calling a real job yet? Votra knew that Vendi didn't necessarily mirror their parents' feelings, but she knew he was reporting everything back to them. She supposed she should be grateful that they were asking after her at all, but a secret, selfish part of her didn't want them to know a single thing about her life.

"I am still working on it, yes." She sat back, snapping the first aid kit shut and placing it on the coffee table. "I managed to hire another person, too."

"Yeah? How is that going?"

She struggled to string together the right combination of words to describe Candy. If she were talking about the purely professional side of it, Candy was fantastic. The work she'd done on the app was invaluable, and there finally seemed to be an end in sight.

But there was so much more to her than that. "It has been good," Votra settled with. "My employee is a very hard worker. We have a launch event in two weeks, and until then, we are just adding some finishing touches to the app."

"Wow. You got a lot done fast." Vendi flexed the hand of her injured arm, a wince flashing across their features. "That is impressive."

He leaned back into the couch cushions, his face a little paler than it was when he first walked in. Wordlessly, Votra went to the kitchen for painkillers. Gods only knew Vendi wouldn't actually ask for them.

"How are you liking working with someone else?" Vendi was just fishing for dirt to pass on to their parents now.

And she fell for it. She was bursting to talk about Candy—Qaed had been her only sounding board for the last few weeks, and his responses never changed.

"Just ask her out" was his go to response. "Go on a date, and if it doesn't work out, then it doesn't work out." Which sounded so much simpler than it really was.

Vendi and Votra were alike in that way. Vendi had never been in a romantic relationship—at least, not one that Votra knew about—and tended to keep to himself. There weren't many people in the world Vendi trusted, and he wouldn't judge Votra for being the same way.

But maybe Candy didn't want Votra talking about her. Votra exhaled. "It has been fine. As I said, she is a hard worker." She trailed her thumb over her knuckles. "She is a good person. I... am very glad that I found her."

"What is her name?"

"Candy." She said it a little too quickly, a little too excitedly. "Why?"

"Just wondering." Vendi shrugged a shoulder. "I would like to meet her one day."

"You will meet her at the launch party." The launch party that was approaching faster than either of them were ready for. The launch party that marked the end of their working relationship, of their... whatever this was.

Votra's blood ran cold, as if she'd been dunked in a vat of ice water. She needed to talk to Candy about their future, if there was one. It had been so easy to get lost in the euphoria of the last few days with her, waking up with Candy in her arms, having the best sex she'd had in her life.

Votra wasn't sure she could do casual anymore. Gods, she'd almost told Candy she loved her in the middle of sex yesterday. But Candy was new to Kratos, new to being single. Maybe, in the grand scheme of things, Votra was just a blip on her radar. She would be honored to be that blip, but she hoped that she was more than that.

"Are you two together?" Vendi's words weren't accusing, but they made Votra feel like she was under a microscope.

She didn't know how to answer that question. She smoothed a hand over the back of her head. They weren't... right? "I am not sure," she said, her voice small.

"Just be careful, alright? I know how you can be sometimes, and I do not want to see you hurt again." She gave Votra's thin thigh a squeeze.

Candy wouldn't hurt her... right? They wouldn't fall into that easy pattern of doing nothing but working, slowly but surely realizing that they were bringing out the worst in each other. They wouldn't crawl into bed at night, still fighting about some little squabble that had broken out in the office earlier because they were both at their wits' end.

Right?

What if that *was* the future that they had to look forward to? If their relationship continued beyond the party, was it all downhill from there?

Vendi's comm beeped loudly, forcibly dragging Votra out of her mental spiral.

"Ah. It is Dad," he said, sending Votra a wary look. "Have you talked to either of them recently?"

The question was innocent enough, but it stoked the fire of irritation simmering in the pit of her stomach. She was so sure Vendi had given up on his plan to smooth things over between Votra and their parents, but apparently, she was wrong.

For the last few years, Vendi's time away from work was typically spent trying to trap Votra and their parents together, in the hopes of repairing their relationship.

But what Vendi didn't know was that there was no going back. Not from this. She'd tried so hard to keep Vendi safe from the knowledge of what their parents were capable of, and she wasn't about to give that up any time soon. She didn't need to know that their parents had ignored every birthday message and every two in the morning call when Votra was so overcome by how much she missed them that maybe, just maybe, she could try again. In Vendi's eyes, their parents were infallible, and she hoped she would never lose that.

"No. I have not," she said a little more sharply than she intended. She didn't want Vendi to know that they weren't coming to the launch party.

Vendi squirmed a little in his seat. "You should come back to Alqen with me to see them. Maybe seeing you will soften them up a little."

Votra didn't believe that for a second. Their parents had made their choices pretty clear years ago. "Thank you for trying, Vendi, but it will not work. I believe that I have done enough trying for one lifetime."

"A lifetime? That is—"

"I do not want to talk about this anymore." Votra's heart pounded aggressively, as if it might force its way past her ribs.

And this was where things would go downhill. Votra could immediately feel her guard going up, and she knew Vendi was going to pummel her with rebuttal after rebuttal. That would inevitably piss Votra off, they'd fight, and Vendi would storm out. They wouldn't talk again until the inevitable year between Vendi's Kratos visits passed, and it would be as if nothing ever happened.

People are good, Votra. Candy's voice echoed in her head. Vendi *was* one of the good ones. All she wanted was to see her family together; Votra couldn't imagine it was easy to be stuck between opposing sides. And more often than not, she chose Votra first.

You just have to believe in the ones that prove their goodness to you.

Votra took in as deep of a breath as her lungs could handle. "I know what you are trying to do, and I appreciate it. I am sorry that you spend so much of your time trying to fix everything. But you do not have to." She rested a hand on Vendi's cheek, and she froze at the very uncharacteristic gesture.

She still didn't want to tell him everything—that was between her and their parents. But maybe she could let him in a little. "I do not think they will come around. But that does not mean that I begrudge you a relationship with them. I am not offended that you are staying with them while you are here."

Vendi blinked, wracking his brain for a response. "What has gotten into you, *ziq'al?*" he asked, the corner of his lips quirking into an uncomfortable smile. "You are making me nervous."

Votra clicked her tongue, giving Vendi's cheek a light smack. "Rude child. I am trying to be nice to you."

"If I am a child, then you are an old woman." Vendi softened a little against Votra's hand. "For the record, I hope that you are wrong. Surely, they will change their minds one day."

Votra wanted to hope so, too. But hope was hard to come by these days. "Maybe."

Vendi rose, stretching his good arm above his head. "I suppose I should go and see them. I told them I was coming into the galaxy quite a while ago, and they will wonder where I am."

"Right." Votra's chest tightened, and her eyes flicked down to Vendi's arm. "Would you like me to drop you off at home?"

"No, that is not necessary. I have driven with one arm many times. I can handle it." Vendi smoothed a hand over her bandaged arm. "Keep me updated about your app, alright? If there is anything I can do for you, do not hesitate to let me know. I mean it."

Asking Vendi for anything felt akin to having a finger chopped off, but Votra nodded anyway. "Thank you. Please be safe getting home. There is only so much I can do as far as injuries go, and I do not think I could help you after a shuttle crash."

Vendi rolled her eyes. "So dramatic." She gave Votra's shoulder a squeeze. "I will see you again soon, I promise."

Votra was already looking forward to it.

Chapter Eighteen

Candy

THAT WAS IT. CANDY had officially scared Votra off.

The entire time they'd worked together, she'd never known Votra not to be there before Candy. She entertained the idea for a second that Votra was just running a little late, but she was pretty sure the word *late* wasn't in Votra's vocabulary.

She'd sent Votra a couple of teasing comm messages, asking her where she was, but they'd all gone unanswered. And now, she was just plain worried.

Her last resort was to message Qaed.

> hiiii uh is votra okay? shes not here and its stressing me out a little

> My apologies, I am not at home at the moment. She is not at work? Let me try to call her.

She didn't allow herself the nosy luxury of asking why Qaed wasn't at home so early in the morning.

> Hm. She did not answer me, either.

> I can get home quickly and check on her.

Candy wanted to check on her. God, when had she become such a worrywart?

> its okay, i'm gonna head over now

Was this crazy, showing up at Votra's apartment just because she was an hour late to work? Maybe it was. Maybe she needed to settle down. But if Qaed was also worried... then she wasn't wrong. She let out a loud groan that echoed throughout the incredibly empty office. If she didn't answer her comm the second time, she'd go.

Candy tried to call her again, and the call went unanswered. "Okay, Votra, I guess we're really doing this," she said, calling a shuttle taxi.

It picked her up a few minutes later, and the second she got in, she felt stupid. Votra was a grown woman who could make her own decisions, and if that decision meant sleeping in an extra hour, so be it.

Candy hadn't worried like this about someone in a long time. Even if this sort of thing had happened with Ross when they were together, she would probably make the assumption that he was ignoring her to play games with his friends.

Or that he was out with some other girl.

The thought flickered through her brain for a split second before fizzling out. Weirdly, she couldn't bring herself to entertain the thought for long. She trusted Votra. It wasn't like they were exclusive or anything, but Candy wasn't really looking to sleep with anyone else. Hell, she was hardly looking to spend *time* with anyone else.

And some little niggling feeling inside her made her think that Votra felt the same way.

Or maybe it was just wishful thinking. Votra was her own woman, and she could do whatever she wanted. After all, the 'no fucking' clause was back on track. They'd fucked well over 'a time or two,' and Votra probably wanted to put her head down for the next two weeks and finish what needed to be finished before the launch party.

Maybe this was selfish, to be pouring her feelings out to Votra while they were in the throes of preparing for the launch of Starcrossed. But she didn't think she could hold it in anymore. Every time she was anywhere near Votra, she felt like she was going to burst at the seams with all of the feelings she had for her.

But the worst Votra could do was deny her. They were contractually bound to work together until the party, so at least she wouldn't lose her job. And if Votra *did* deny her, then she'd just go back to Earth and live with her parents, or she'd get her own apartment in Brooklyn. With a cat. A cat would be cool.

But going back home didn't sound as good as it used to.

The taxi dropped her off in front of Votra's apartment, and flashbacks of all those fucking *stairs* came flooding back to her. God, this better be worth it.

Votra was *actually* going to think she was crazy, getting her address from Qaed to come and make sure she was alright. What if Votra was on her way to work right now and she got to work and Candy wasn't there?

Candy didn't have much time to overthink it. The door opened a moment later, and Candy couldn't bring herself to look up. Every word she'd rehearsed in her head in the taxi shuttle on the way over evaded her, but maybe Votra would find it charming that she was speaking directly from the heart.

"Sorry, I know there is probably a reason that you didn't come to work this morning and I'm totally overstepping a boundary by being here. I just wanted to check on you and I also just really wanted to tell you that, when I said that I liked you at Felicette yesterday, I meant it. Like, more than just the whole sleeping together thing. I mean, I like that too, of course. I'd be really fucking stupid not to like that part. But I also like being around you and—"

"Let me get Votra for you." The voice that interrupted her was a good amount deeper than Votra's, tinged with an amusement that Candy felt in her bones. She forced her gaze up to a qintaril who was somehow even taller than Votra. His skin was the same pretty blue-gray, but that was where their similarities ended. His shoulders were broad and his chest even broader, muscular arms barely contained by the t-shirt he wore. One of their arms was bandaged tightly.

Shit. Her sibling. Candy grabbed his arm before he could turn. "Please don't," she said quickly. "Don't tell her what I just said. This kind of just feels like it wasn't supposed to happen."

Votra's sibling glanced down at Candy's hand. "You are Candy, right?" she asked, and the hairs on the back of Candy's neck stood on end.

Votra talked about her? "Yeah, I am."

"I do not think you have anything to worry about." Vendi patted Candy's hand, and she relinquished her hold on him. "You should come in, at least. I know she would be happy to see you."

She was too weak of a human to say no to an opportunity to see Votra. "Okay," she said meekly, following her into the apartment.

Votra's eyes were on her the second she stepped in. Shit, had she heard all of that anyway? "Hi," Candy said, voice more akin to a squeak.

"Hi." Candy couldn't read the expression on Votra's face.

This was stupid. "Sorry, I should probably go—"

"It is alright. I was just leaving." Vendi patted Votra's shoulder, and they exchanged glances that Candy didn't understand. "I will be in the galaxy for a while, though. Perhaps the three of us could get lunch some time."

"That would be nice," Candy said, stealing the occasional glance at Votra. She genuinely couldn't tell if she'd heard anything that she'd said to Vendi, or if she had, how she felt about it. She just looked... tired.

Oh God. Had she just interrupted something between them and now they had to act like everything was fine because she was here?

"It is so nice to see that you have found someone so good for you, Votra," Vendi said, resting her hand on the doorknob. "I would have thought you would be more excited to introduce her to me."

"I–" Votra cleared her throat. "Candy and I are not... *together.*"

Candy's body ran hot and cold at the same time. Sure, it was true, but... hearing it out loud so casually felt... bad. *Candy and I just work together and I don't even know why she came all the way over here.*

This was what she got for jumping into something with the first alien that gave her any sort of attention. Apparently, aliens and humans weren't so different after all. Votra was just another person who was ashamed of her–but this time, she really couldn't place why. She'd had a rebuttal against every wall Candy had thrown up.

Vendi stopped, his hand stilling on the doorknob. "Really? I would not have guessed."

Candy just wanted to leave. She wanted to go home, crawl into her bed, and cry. She wanted *her* bed, not the bed back at Xyxy's. "Yeah. I was just coming to check on her since she didn't come to work. But, uh, apparently everything's okay."

Vendi's gaze didn't waver from Votra. "Apparently so." She opened the door, and Candy had half a mind to dart out after her. "It was lovely to meet you, Candy. Think about that lunch, okay?" Votra still didn't say a word as the door closed behind her.

She sucked in a deep, shuddering breath, not looking at Votra. Her face tingled with heat, anger seeping through her pores. "Wow. This was stupid. I, uh... I should go."

"Wait, what is wrong?" Votra's voice was small, distant. God, that pissed Candy off. So *now* she could talk?

"Nothing. I think I was just... reading too far into this. This is on me." It wasn't like Votra was wrong. They *weren't* together. And maybe Candy was naive for feeling like they were.

"Candy, wait–"

Candy drew in a shuddering breath. "I just wanted to make sure you were alive, because you, like, *never* miss work. And you're alive. So... I can go." More than anything, she was embarrassed. Embarrassed to be having this big of a reaction to something so small–she'd fallen too hard, too fast, as always, and she had no one to blame but herself.

She had to learn how to exercise some form of self-preservation, because God only knew she'd never been good at it in the past. She didn't have the excuse of being with Votra for five years to keep her here.

It was two weeks of her life. And she could throw that away if it meant keeping her heart safe.

She left before Votra had the chance to stop her. There. She'd done it. She'd stood up for herself, because dammit, she deserved it.

The rain seeping into every fiber of her clothing only made matters worse. It was raining harder now. Veterok-III's rain was ice cold, stinging her skin like tiny shards of glass.

And she hadn't even called a fucking taxi. "God dammit," she muttered, angry, hot tears streaming down her cheeks. At least they were keeping her face kind of warm. She weaved through all of those fucking staircases, and right now, she hated Votra for living in such a stupid place.

She wrapped her arms around herself as she stood in the parking area, surrounded by shuttles but none of which could take her out of here.

"Candy!" Votra's voice broke through her thoughts as she tapped her wet comm screen to call a taxi.

For a second, the sound of Votra's voice excited her. She wiped the tears and salty rainwater from her eyes and briefly wondered how long she could pretend like she hadn't heard her.

"Did I say something that bothered you?" Candy's back was still to Votra, and she half expected Votra to grab her and spin her around. But she didn't. She stood close enough to make herself heard over the rain, but didn't intrude. "Please talk to me."

Candy wiped the rain from her eyes with the heels of her palms. Votra *did* sound like she genuinely didn't know what she had done wrong, and Candy couldn't tell if that pissed her off or made her feel better. "You didn't say anything wrong. You were right. We're *not* together, so there's no reason for me to be all dramatic about it."

Votra went silent for a beat, the steady thrumming of the rain the only sound between them. "...Did it bother you that I told Vendi we are not together?"

Candy swallowed back the stubborn lump forming in the back of her throat. "Yeah. It did. And there's no reason for it to because we *aren't* together but hearing it out loud–" A strangled sob cut her off, and she clamped a hand over her quivering lips. "God. Why can't I call a fucking taxi?"

"Do not call one." Votra spoke even louder as the rain picked up. "Please talk to me, Candy. Truly, I did not know you felt that way."

"Of course I do!" Candy snapped, whipping around to face Votra. Yule was right–Votra *was* clueless. If she weren't so pissed, she'd find it endearing. "I told you I liked you back at the restaurant! I keep trying to be a part of your life outside that fucking office and you keep not letting me! You'll let me in enough to have sex with me but you don't want me more than that?"

"I *do* want you more than that, Candy. More than I know how to tell you." Votra sighed, smoothing her hands over her eyes to clear the water streaming down her face. "I am so, *so* deeply terrified of how badly I want you in every capacity. But the last time I felt like this for someone–"

"I'm not going to steal your work, Votra," Candy snapped, and Votra visibly recoiled. "I've cared about you from the second I met you at Xyxy's party and I feel like I've done a pretty fucking good job of showing you that you can trust me."

"Zeele did not steal my work. I gave it to her." Candy's lips parted in surprise as Votra continued. "She brought out the worst in me. She is like me—married to her work. If you think *I* neglect my health in favor of work, you would hate to see Zeele when she is focused. I slept in the office every night, and the second I woke up, I was back at my desk. And we did that together for years.

"But we fought. A lot, as sleep deprived, malnourished people tend to do." She swallowed, ducking her head if only for a reprieve from the rain. "We were terrible for each other. And one day, she grew tired of it. She told me that she was leaving, and I told her that she could use the base code of Starcrossed for her own app. And then she brought LoveNet out a week later."

"She didn't build an entire app in a week."

"I know." Votra's eyes glittered with tears as she lifted her head to look at Candy again. "Our relationship was so tumultuous, so stressful, but I still loved her so much that I was willing to give her whatever she asked for. But you are so... so truly good, and you bring so much joy to my life. And I am scared that I would give you the world if you asked for it."

A sob made its way past Candy's lips, and she let herself be pulled into Votra's arms. "I don't need anything from you," she muttered into the soaked fabric of her shirt. "I wanna be with you because you make me feel *safe*. You make me feel like you want me, like, *actually* want me for exactly who I am. I don't have to be some watered down version of myself."

"I *do* want you. Every part of you," Votra said, taking Candy's face into her hands. "I love everything that makes you, you. Every tear, every ridiculously loud laugh. Those are the things I fell for."

"And I fell for the Votra who talked my ear off about *Outlaw Koran* on my best friend's balcony in the middle of a party." Candy's lower lip wobbled. "I don't want you because of Starcrossed, Votra. I love Starcrossed, but also, *fuck* Starcrossed." Votra flinched at that, and Candy laughed a weak, watery laugh. "I would love you if you woke up tomorrow and told me you never wanted to look at Starcrossed again. We would make it work. Because I'm in this for *you*, and nothing else."

"So... if I woke up tomorrow morning and told you I *did* want to keep working on Starcrossed... love is off the table?" Votra's voice was teasing, but hot tears rolled down her cheeks, mingling with the salty rainwater.

Candy laughed, really laughed this time. "You're such a pain in the ass," she said, balling her fists into Votra's shirt.

Votra smoothed her thumbs across Candy's cheeks. "Will you promise me something?" she asked.

"Anything."

"Promise me you will not grow tired of me," she whispered, her voice breaking under the weight of her vulnerability. "I know that I work too much and I know that it is hard to pull me out of it. I know that I hyperfixate and forget to eat or sleep and I do not know how to control that. It is not for a lack of caring about you or wanting to be around you–"

"Votra." Candy pressed herself against Votra's torso, leaning in as close as she could. "I've got you, okay? I'm not going to get tired of you. I'm gonna be right next to you, forcing you to take breaks to eat and rest. And occasionally, to have sex with me." Votra laughed, once again wiping the rain from her face. "We're in this together. Because I... I love you."

The next thing she knew, her feet weren't on the ground anymore. Votra lifted her, arms securely around Candy's upper thighs, and kissed her. The pressure of her still tender thighs against Votra's firm body stung a little. Candy whimpered against Votra's lips, and she pulled back a little. "Are you alright?"

"Yes. Don't you dare put me down." Her hands found Votra's cheeks and she kissed her again. Candy couldn't tell where the salty rainwater began and her tears ended.

Votra peppered kisses all over Candy's damp face. "I love you, too," she whispered once her lips found their way to the shell of Candy's ear.

Candy shivered violently, the combination of being chilled to the bone and Votra's mouth against her ear proving almost lethal. "Can we go inside now?" she asked.

"Please."

Chapter Nineteen

Votra

THERE WAS NO POINT in trying to stay in the rain-soaked clothes that were now plastered to Votra's skin. She struggled with her already tight shirt the moment they crossed the threshold of Votra's apartment, and Candy giggled breathlessly as she helped her tug it off. "Oh my God, you're even colder than you usually are," she laughed, pressing her frigid hands to Votra's chest.

Normally, Candy's hands were warmer than the rest of Votra's body, but they felt surprisingly cold against her. "So are you, poor thing," Votra murmured, trembling fingers fumbling with the buttons of Candy's blouse. Her hands were practically useless at this point. She tugged at either side of Candy's shirt, hoping the buttons would simply pop free, but instead, the top two buttons came off completely, ricocheting off the wall behind them.

Candy swore under her breath, capturing her lower lip between her teeth. "You can do that again whenever you want."

"I am not trying to get in the habit of destroying your clothes," Votra laughed, dipping her head to press a kiss to the goose pimpled flesh of Candy's chest.

"I don't mind. It was kinda hot." Candy peeled off her blouse and dropped it to the floor at her feet, leaving her in a soaked bra that didn't look even remotely comfortable. "Is there any chance you're in the market for a shower? I smell like outside."

Votra's mouth returned to Candy's skin, this time ghosting her lips across her collarbone. "I could take a shower." A shower with Candy sounded like the best thing in the world right now. She pried herself away from Candy just long enough to lead her through the hallway past the living room into the bathroom attached to her bedroom.

She turned the shower on, setting the water a good amount hotter than she generally liked. Candy peeled off the rest of her clothing, revealing milky white thighs that were free of any remnants of what had happened the day before, save for a bandage on her outer thigh.

"Gods, you are beautiful," she breathed, greedily snatching Candy into her arms again.

Candy giggled, brushing her nose against Votra's jaw. "As much as I love being complimented, I really wanna get into this shower before I die of hypothermia."

"So dramatic." But Votra released her, pulling off her slacks and underwear as Candy got into the shower. She let out a loud sigh of relief at the stream of hot water against her back.

"Come here." Candy reached her hands out for Votra and she climbed into the shower with her. The first thing Candy did once Votra was close enough was drag her down for a kiss.

She could get used to this. Having Candy in her bedroom, in her *shower*, felt a bit like she was laying her soul bare in front of her. And strangely, she didn't hate it. Being known, being seen, felt nice.

Votra's hands wandered down Candy's wet torso, settling on her hips. "So, why did you come over here in the first place?" she asked, moving back a little to press her back to the cool tile of the shower wall.

Candy followed her, moving forward to press herself flush against Votra. Votra bit back a groan at the feeling of her half-hard cock against Candy's soft stomach. "Because you were an hour late for work and I hadn't heard from you," Candy started, starting a languid trail of kisses down Votra's neck. "And the Votra I know doesn't miss work like that."

"I am missing work now," she pointed out, voice strained as Candy's lips made their way back to her jaw.

"Smart ass." She pushed herself up on her toes to kiss Votra again. "I was worried about you. And then somehow, I talked myself into confessing my feelings to you after I made sure you were still, y'know, alive."

Votra captured Candy's chin between two fingers. "I apologize for worrying you," she said. Candy smiled, melting into Votra's touch. "And... for everything with Vendi. I did not realize that what I said might hurt you."

"It's okay." Votra drew Candy in again, only for Candy to stop, lips hovering over Votra's. "I may or may not have confessed my feelings to Vendi before all that happened, which... definitely made the crash out a little worse."

"To Vendi?" Votra blinked.

"Well, I confessed my feelings to Vendi because I thought they were you. Which is weird, because they're *way* less hot than you."

Votra didn't try to restrain her bark of laughter. "Gods, I do not think I have ever heard anyone say that before."

"Well, it's true. Nothing against Vendi, of course." Candy's teeth raked over her lower lip. "You're so pretty. Have I told you that before?"

Oh, she had. Many times. And it made her cock twitch every time. She knew Candy could feel her hardening against her, and that was probably exactly why she was doing this. "What *did* you say to Vendi?" Votra pushed Candy's soaked bangs from her eyes, her human's skin hot against her now.

"Wouldn't you like to know?" Her eyes sparkled with mischief, her hand falling down to Votra's rock hard member. Votra sucked in a sharp breath. "Maybe I'll tell you later. For now, I think I've earned the right to give you a little bit of a hard time."

Votra didn't know what Candy was going to do, but the anticipation sent a shiver through her. "I cannot argue with that," she said through gritted teeth, pushing her hips selfishly into Candy's fist.

Candy pumped her hand agonizingly slowly down Votra's length, and Votra leaned her head back against the shower wall. "I'm gonna touch you until you're begging for me to let you come," she said, pressing a kiss to the corner of Votra's mouth. "And you're going to have to do a *lot* of begging before I say yes."

Fuck. Votra's cock was already weeping for attention at Candy's words alone. "Candy," she whimpered, her breath hitching as Candy brushed her thumb over Votra's slit.

And just as quickly as Candy took her into her hand, she pulled back. "You probably don't have shampoo, do you? Neither you or Qaed have hair.... Damn. My hair reeks."

Votra's head was swimming from the heady combination of the steam filling the room and the arousal pounding through her body. She thought for a moment about taking her cock into her hand, if only to find out what Candy would do if she did.

"I will keep some here for you," Votra said. "If you would like."

"Okay, but I'll bring it over. I'm *very* specific about what I put in my hair." A small smile tugged at Candy's suddenly very pink lips. "That's very considerate of you. Thank you, honey." She slid onto her knees, skating her hands along Votra's thighs. One of her hands circled the base of Votra's cock, and it took all of her restraint not to shove herself into Candy's mouth.

Candy took her into her mouth slowly, starting with only the head and swirling her hot, wet tongue around it. Votra grunted, fisting her hand into Candy's wet hair. It was embarrassing, how close she was already. But there was something about being intimate with Candy, knowing how she felt about her, that made it so much better.

"Candy—" Votra choked out, which immediately proved to be a mistake. Candy pulled her mouth away with a gentle *pop*, a smirk playing across her lips.

"Sorry. It's kind of hard to do this in the shower," she said, flattening her tongue against the underside of Votra's desperate cock and giving it one long, teasing lick before standing again.

Gods, Votra wasn't going to survive this. Her orgasm coiled in the pit of her stomach, waiting to be set free, but Candy seemed to have no intention of letting that happen. She leaned into Votra, pinning her erection between them, and Votra thought she might come just from that. "Are you close, honey?" Candy purred, nipping at the sensitive skin of her jaw.

"Yes," Votra whined, pressing herself into Candy's stomach.

Candy immediately pulled away. "I need to wash my body. I stink like rain." She helped herself to a hearty squeeze of Votra's body wash, Votra's heart constricting at how intimate that felt. Her psyche was trapped in a rollercoaster of emotions, but the only constant was that she was constantly getting more aroused.

She worked the body wash into a lather, the suds streaming down her body, sliding between her legs, down her ample ass. Votra had never been so jealous of soap in her entire life. She reached for Candy and was immediately stopped by a hand encircling her wrist. "Be patient. You'll get your turn with me later."

Votra watched as Candy rinsed the soap from her body, wanton groans mingling with her labored breaths. She took her time with herself, trailing her hands over her breasts to rid them of soap. "Candy, please," she whimpered. She didn't even really know what she was asking for. She just wanted *her*.

"I told you I was gonna make you beg for it, honey," Candy said, shutting off the water once she was free of soap. Votra could already tell that *honey* was going to cause a problem for her. The word made her dick stir, and for a moment, she was sure she was going to come without being touched.

She took one of Votra's towels from the rail on the wall, leaning into Votra to wrap it around her waist. She palmed Votra's length against the towel, and Votra cursed under her breath. "Want me to take you to bed?" she asked.

"Gods, yes," Votra said embarrassingly fast. She dried herself off as quickly as she could, her eyes trained on Candy as she rubbed a towel over her own body. Despite how damp her body was, her mouth was completely dry.

They moved into Votra's bedroom and Votra tried once again to touch Candy in whatever capacity she could. But still, Candy denied her. "Get on the bed," she said coolly, and she had no choice but to obey. She pressed her back against the headboard of her bed and Candy crawled between her legs.

"Good girl." Candy slid her hands up Votra's thighs. Votra's need had waned a little as they moved into the bedroom, but Candy's soft hands on her reawakened it. She moved into Votra's lap, thick thighs flanking her hips as she pressed her wet, throbbing heat against Votra's dick.

And Votra was immediately swallowed by the need to fuck her senseless. "Fuck, you feel so good," Votra choked out, reaching her hands out to cup Candy's ass.

"Well, you're not gonna feel much of this yet. I'm gonna fuck myself on you, and you're just gonna watch." Candy's eyes locked with Votra's as she moved against her, sliding herself along Votra's length.

"Shit," Candy breathed. "Your cock is amazing, have I ever told you that? It feels so fucking good against me." She took Votra into her hand and trailed her tip along her slick pussy, teasing herself. She positioned herself like she was going to take Votra inside her, but Votra wasn't sure she was going to be that lucky just yet.

And she was right. Candy released her, sliding her hand between her legs instead. "Just think, this could be you inside me instead of my fingers," she murmured, pushing a single finger inside of herself.

Votra could hardly think straight. "Please... let me be inside you," she pleaded, shamelessly bucking her hips into the air. Frustration crested in her, her forgotten release blossoming in the pit of her stomach.

"Tell me how bad you want it." Candy introduced another finger and gasped against it, grinding her hips into her own hand. That should be *Votra.*

"I *need* it. I need *you,*" Votra gasped. "Please, Candy. Let me apologize to you properly. Let me make you feel better than you have ever felt in your life."

Candy removed her hand from herself with a little groan. "Yeah? You're gonna fuck an apology into me?" She took Votra's cock into her hands, and she was all too aware of Candy's slick fingers against her. "Go ahead then. Do it."

Votra was more than happy to accept the challenge. Candy slid down onto Votra's length, her already stretched pussy taking her almost immediately.

The feeling of Candy's walls tightening around her choked the words Votra was trying so hard to get out. Votra sunk her fingertips into Candy's bare hips, gripping her as she pistoned in and out of her.

Fuck, she wasn't going to last long like this. Her orgasm had been looming for so long, even the smallest bit of contact from Candy drove her mad.

Candy's eyes locked onto Votra's, the pleasure flashing in those beautiful green eyes sending a thrill through her. "Oh *fuck,* I'm gonna come," Candy moaned, and crashed her lips against Votra's. She let out a stream of desperate moans into Votra's mouth, and Votra couldn't keep herself from falling over the edge, pulling out just in time to coat Candy's glistening chest with her cum. Candy's orgasm came shortly after, and Votra relished the feeling of it coating her thigh.

"Alright, fine, I forgive you," Candy huffed, resting her forehead against Votra's. A small smile tugged at her lips. "Unless you wanna try that apology again."

Votra wouldn't move right now if someone paid her to. "Well, we have all day." She kissed Candy firmly, smoothing her thumb over Candy's hip. "Let me try again. At least once more."

"You can try as many times as you want."

Chapter Twenty

Votra

TWO WEEKS LATER

Votra was endlessly grateful that Candy ended up spending the night before the launch party, because the only thing that managed to ground her was waking up entangled in the limbs of the most beautiful creature she'd ever laid eyes on. She'd stolen one of Votra's very few t-shirts, and Votra didn't think she'd ever have the heart to take it back.

She let Candy sleep, sneaking out of the bedroom as quietly as she could and closing the door carefully behind her. If she stayed in the bedroom, she'd just end up restlessly wandering around the room, trying to find something to do with herself.

If she were alone, she would have gone to the office. But it wasn't just about her now. And anyway, she wasn't sure she could bring herself to leave Candy alone, especially not today.

She trudged into the kitchen and started on a pot of coffee–she kept it around now, having developed a bit of a dependency on it since Candy started bringing it in most mornings. She hadn't developed much of a finesse to making it beyond chucking the grounds into a paper filter and dumping an estimation of hot water over it, but it did the trick.

"I am surprised to see you here," came Qaed's sleep-graveled voice. He yawned, a hand coming up to scratch his chest. Her eyes shifted to the long, shiny scar that stretched from the base of his throat to the middle of his chest. Somehow, she still hadn't gotten used to seeing it yet.

"Candy is here," Votra said, watching Qaed as he pulled a mug from the cupboard and placed it next to Votra's. She added another scoop of grounds to the filter and poured more water over them. "She sleeps like the dead."

"She spent the night?" Qaed leaned against the counter, arms over his chest as Votra poured the coffee into both of their mugs. "Why?"

Qaed knew fully well why Candy had spent the night. But it was up to her to say it now. She owed Candy that much. "I have not asked her for titles, but... we are together." Warmth blossomed in her chest, and she ducked her head to hide the smile stretching her lips. "Which you would know if you ever spent the night at home."

"Hey, do not turn this around on me." Qaed dumped an ungodly amount of sugar into his coffee, and briefly, Votra regretted making it for him. Surely his poor, weakened heart wouldn't be able to handle much more of this. She plucked the sugar container from his hands once she reached a point of not being able to stand by in good conscience anymore. "Good. That means Vendi owes me fifty credits."

"Fifty credits?"

"We were taking bets on whether you and Candy were together or not. Vendi did not think so, but I know you." He grinned. "I am happy for you. Candy is lovely, she really is. *Certainly* a step up from your last relationship."

Votra scoffed. "More than a step." She leaned back against the counter next to him, nursing her mug between her hands. "Do you think that Zeele is going to show up at the launch party?"

"I would be doing you a disservice if I said no. You know she is going to want to know what you are doing." Qaed shifted towards her, resting his arm against hers. "But it will be alright. You will have Candy with you. And me." He tugged Votra's head to rest against his shoulder, resting a comforting hand on the side of her head. Generally, she wasn't the biggest fan of physical affection, but Qaed's touch quelled her nerves. "How are you feeling?"

Terrified. Votra was fighting a losing battle with her nervous system, which seemed to want to worm its way out of her body. But "nervous" was what she settled with. "I did not sleep last night because I could not stop thinking about what could go wrong."

"What could go wrong?" Qaed asked. "Starcrossed is already so beloved by everyone who has tested it. All you have to do is show up and allow everyone to tell you how fantastic you are."

Votra took a sip of her coffee, averting Qaed's gaze. She wasn't particularly in the mood to rehash all of her feelings about her family, but Qaed was no stranger to what her parents were like. She didn't have to explain anything to him. "Does it sound ungrateful to say that being praised by strangers also sounds rather awful?"

"A little bit. But knowing you, it is unsurprising." He chuckled. "Is Vendi coming?"

Vendi was probably at their parents' house right now. Votra's chest ached at the thought of them eating breakfast together, her parents more than delighted that their favorite child had come back to visit. How lucky for them that it wasn't their other child, their failure child. The child who wasted her time on something as flimsy as love.

The beginnings of tears tickled Votra's sinuses, but she was distracted by the creak of a door opening. Candy shuffled into the kitchen in nothing but Votra's shirt and the cute pink underwear Votra had reveled in pulling off her last night. Her eyes were heavy-lidded with sleep, and a yawn stretched her pink lips before her eyes snapped open.

"Shit, Qaed! I forgot you—" Candy grimaced, possibly not wanting to confess to Qaed she forgot he lived here. She didn't try to cover herself up, but Qaed politely shifted his gaze away from her. "Sorry. I just woke up. I promise it wasn't my goal to show you my ass first thing in the morning."

"It is alright. If I looked like you, I would be walking around without pants on as well."

"Aww, thanks," Candy cooed, any trace of shyness completely disappearing. "You're looking pretty good yourself. You work out?" She squeezed one of his biceps and he flexed it for her.

"Occasionally," Qaed said. She knew he was actually enjoying this—the one tenet of his life as a bounty hunter that he'd clung to since his forced retirement was staying in shape.

Candy finally relinquished her hold on Qaed and shifted her attention to Votra, plucking the mug from her hands and taking a sip. She immediately made a face. "Ugh, I forgot you drink this without anything in it. Could you make me some?"

"Of course, *ta'qel*," Votra said, and immediately froze. Had she actually said that out loud? Qaed's eyes snapped to Votra, but if Candy noticed, she didn't say anything.

She'd come so close to uttering that word so many times now, but this was the first time it had actually slipped out. And it felt... nice. She'd never felt even close to comfortable calling someone by that word, but it felt like it was meant for Candy.

Votra poured Candy's mug and passed it to her with the sugar. Qaed shot her a pointed look, and something told her she was going to hear about this later. But maybe, if she was lucky, Qaed wouldn't want to stress her out before the launch party.

"To answer your question, yes. Vendi is coming," Votra said quickly, in the hopes of steering Qaed's conversation away from her slip. "I told him about it yesterday."

"She is still in Kratos?" Qaed asked, watching Candy as she dumped nearly as much sugar into her mug of coffee. Votra was surrounded by monsters.

Votra chewed her lip. "She is... taking a break." Concern flashed across Qaed's face. "Maybe you can ask her about it at the party."

Qaed seemed to get the message. "Right. Yes, I will." He cleared his throat, pushing himself away from the counter. "Alright, I am going to go and get ready. I promised Xyxy and Yule I would come and help them prepare the venue for tonight, and from Xyxy's message, I am assuming she has quite a lot planned for me."

"Let us know if you need anything," Candy said, clutching her mug between both hands.

"No. You two stay here and relax until the party. Tonight is a big night for you both, and you should be as rested as possible." Votra didn't miss the fact that Qaed stared directly at her as he spoke. "I will see you both tonight."

She hated to admit it, but Votra was grateful for a quiet day before the inevitably overstimulating night. And selfishly, she was glad for a day with just Candy before she had to share her with the masses.

Qaed took his coffee to his room, leaving Candy and Votra alone in the kitchen. Candy shuffled closer to Votra and leaned into her. "I can't believe it's tonight," she murmured, staring into her coffee. "Did you prepare your speech?"

"I did. But we will see how well I actually deliver it," she chuckled, taking one more sip of her coffee before putting it back down on the counter. "What should we do with our day before the party?"

Candy pursed her lips. "Well... we have your apartment to ourselves...," she purred, shifting to position herself between Votra's legs. She placed her mug on the counter and stood on her tiptoes, her shirt riding up as she draped her arms lazily around Votra's shoulders. "A little stress relief before the party would probably do us some good, right?"

"I never grow tired of your endless libido," Votra laughed, hooking her hands under Candy's thighs and lifting her into her arms. "I think you are right. If anything, it will help us go into the party much more relaxed."

"Exactly. You read my mind." Candy's lips found the length of Votra's neck, trailing hot, slow kisses down it. "Take me to bed, *ta'qel.*"

Votra felt as if her heart might fling itself out of her body through her throat. "Do you know what that means?" she asked, her voice thin.

"No, but you called me that earlier, so I assumed it was a term of endearment." Candy's eyebrows shot up. "Unless you were secretly calling me a bitch or something."

Votra laughed, making her way back to the bedroom with Candy clinging to her torso. "Not at all." She lowered her mouth to the shell of Candy's ear, and every tiny hair on the back of Candy's neck stood on end. "I will tell you in bed."

She laid Candy gently on her bed, her legs falling open for Votra immediately. Every inch of Candy's body was intoxicating — the delicate curve of her soft stomach peeking out from under the hem of her shirt, the divot in her hips that flared out into thick, luscious thighs. She wanted to worship it all.

So she did. She went down onto her knees and took one of Candy's feet in her hands. Her lips found Candy's ankle, trailed up the length of her calf. "So, you want to know what *ta'qel* means?"

"Yes," Candy gasped, squirming under Votra's touch.

Votra clenched her jaw against the rising tide of emotion swelling in the back of her throat. "Its meaning is a bit more complicated than just one word. It does not have a direct translation in Universal." She nipped the sensitive skin of Candy's inner thigh, earning her a sharp whine. "A qintaril's *ta'qel* is the person that they choose to dedicate their life to. It is not unlike a human's spouse–but we do not necessarily have a ceremony to earn that title. We are bound to our *ta'qel* until death and beyond."

A stubborn tear trailed down Votra's cheek, and she blotted it against Candy's thigh. "We only take one *ta'qel* our entire lives. And I have never felt right saying it to anyone until now. Until you."

"Not even–"

"No. No one." Votra didn't want to hear Zeele's name spoken aloud; not by Candy, not in this room. Never again, if she could. "I will be by your side for as long as you will have me."

"Come up here, you romantic jerk," Candy laughed through tears.

But Votra didn't stop. She continued her trail of worshipping kisses up the length of Candy's body, pushing her shirt up as she moved up Candy's soft torso. She took one of Candy's nipples into her mouth, drawing it to attention against her tongue. Candy whimpered, moving her hips up against Votra's torso that was now settled between her legs. Votra let her, shifting her weight down to give Candy even more to press herself against.

She shifted her attention to the other breast, giving the other nipple just as much attention. Candy clawed at her horns, drawing her thighs up to clamp against Votra's sides. Her beautiful human was putty under the control of her mouth.

She trailed her tongue along Candy's throat, and when their mouths finally reconnected, Candy tasted like coffee. How lucky would she be to have this whenever she wanted? To wake up every day with the love of her life, tasting the morning on her lips?

Votra pulled away, giving herself a moment to burn this memory into her brain. How Candy looked beneath her, hair sprawled out on the pillow around her in a soft, pink halo, skin flushed from her cheeks down to her chest, thighs trembling with want.

"You gonna stare at me all day or fuck me?" Candy whined, her thick thighs still clutching Votra's waist.

Votra exhaled a chuckle. "I was admiring you, my heart," she murmured. "Am I not allowed to look at you?"

Candy's blush deepened, her hands skimming up the length of Votra's stomach. "You can look at me. But I'd like it a lot if you looked at me *and* touched me."

"Touch you where?"

"Everywhere. I just want your hands on me." Candy squirmed beneath her, moving her hips up against her, desperate for friction.

Votra loved seeing her like this. "You have to give me instruction, *ta'qel*. Where do you want my hands?"

"Between my legs." She captured one of Votra's hands in her own, guiding it to her clothed pussy. She was already soaked, her arousal coating Votra's fingers as she pushed her underwear aside and slid her fingers between her folds.

Her grip around Votra's wrist tightened. "Yeah, like that. Fuck me with your fingers," she instructed breathlessly. Votra pushed a finger into her slowly, and her walls immediately clenched around her. Her finger pistoned in and out of her teasingly, and Candy's little whines told her she was getting frustrated.

"More, Votra, I want you to fill me up." She pushed her hips against Votra, desperate for the sensation that only one of Votra's fingers couldn't provide.

Votra liked seeing her come undone like this, wanting more, *needing* more. She rewarded her by introducing a second thick finger, which she immediately cried out at. "Yes, yes, thank you," she gasped, arching her back off the bed. "Fuck me harder, baby, please, *now.*"

Votra thought about teasing her, about making her beg for it like Candy so loved to do to her. But she couldn't bring herself to. She *wanted* to fuck Candy senseless, to leave her so sore that all she'd be thinking about during the launch party was being full of Votra again.

"Anything for you, my love," she purred, and Candy balled the comforter into her fists. She curled the tips of her fingers inside her, brushing the spot that drew the most illicit of moans from Candy.

"There, right there." Candy reached blindly for Votra's hand, her thighs trembling, toes curled as she pressed Votra's palm against her clit. She bucked her hips against her, free hand clamped over her mouth.

That wouldn't do. "Let me hear you, *please*," Votra all but begged, and Candy obliged, moans now spilling free from her kiss-swollen lips.

Votra palmed herself through her pants, every muscle in her body taut with the orgasm that crept closer and closer with every moan from Candy. Candy peered at her through her eyelashes, her lips parted as she gasped for breath.

"My poor baby, so fucking horny she can't help but touch herself." Candy's words were stilted, interrupted by the little sounds of pleasure that she didn't seem to be able to hold back. "I love when you do that. Watching me get fucked by you turns you on *that* much, huh?"

"Yes," Votra moaned. Now that she'd been caught, she took her cock into her hand and stroked it, finally giving herself the attention she'd been so desperate for. There was something she loved about Candy watching her get off, about seeing Candy so turned on by something that made Votra feel incredibly vulnerable.

Candy forced Votra's hand out of her, and she immediately missed the feeling of Candy's walls tightening around her fingers. "Fuck me with your pretty cock, then."

Votra positioned herself over Candy's entrance with a trembling hand, her entire body coiled so tightly she felt like she might burst the second she was inside her. Her already stretched pussy took her so well, and Votra muffled her moans against Candy's lips. Candy drew her legs up and around Votra's waist, locking her into place.

Fuck, she wasn't going to make it at this rate. She rutted her hips against Candy the best she could, her moans mingling with Candy's. She wouldn't mind spending her entire day buried inside Candy, not moving from this bed for a second.

"Tell me to come," Candy cried out, angling her hips to allow her clit to brush against the bundle of hard tissue at the base of Votra's cock. "I wanna come for you."

"Then come. Come all over me, my love," Votra choked out, her stomach tightening with her own impending release. Candy's moans picked up in volume, growing sharper, needier as she came, her release coating Votra entirely. Votra's vision tunneled as she came as well, Candy's tightness milking the seemingly endless supply of cum from her.

Her legs dropped from Votra's waist, but she didn't pull away from her, and Votra didn't dare pull out. Her cock softened inside her, but she kind of liked the feeling of it, of being so close to Candy that they were physically attached to one another.

Votra collapsed on top of Candy, and she grunted at the sudden weight. "Tired?" she teased, trailing her fingertips across the back of her head.

"Not at all." Votra could keep going all day at this rate. Once the post-orgasm sensitivity wore off, the knowledge of her dick still being nestled inside Candy stoked the fires of her arousal. It didn't help that Candy was lazily grinding her hips against her, very clearly not sated either.

"Good. We have a lot of day to kill," Candy said. She reached down to pull Votra's dick from inside her, her beautiful, friction-swollen pussy glistening with a mixture of her release and Votra's. "And you have a mess to clean up."

Now Votra was *definitely* hard. "As you wish."

Hours of distraction sex later, Votra had to force herself out of bed. Their comms had vibrated more times than Votra could count with reminders about the launch party from Xyxy.

The afternoon had definitely been a distraction, but now that the party was only about an hour away, the reality of it was starting to settle in again. They took a shower together to wash away the afternoon's activities, and as they dressed together, Votra found herself disappointed that Candy was covering up the body that Votra had so enjoyed being privy to all day.

But her dress was beautiful. It was a simple blue-gray satin slip dress that fell to her mid calf and clung to her hips. "Can I borrow a blazer from you?" she asked, clipping a small silver star clip into her now dry hair.

"It will be quite large on you," Votra pointed out. She'd purchased a silky pink shirt for the occasion, one that she, as always, didn't button up all the way. She pulled on her favorite black slacks, the ones she'd had for years that had practically melded to her body.

"I know what I'm doing," Candy grinned as she took the blazer from her. Rather than pulling it on all the way, she let it settle on her shoulders and fall like a curtain around her.

She was right. She *did* know what she was doing. "I like how you look in my clothes." Votra slid her hands under the blazer to rest on her hips.

Candy rested her hands on Votra's chest. "And I like you in pink." She rose to brush her lips along Votra's jaw, and she shivered.

"You know, I am starting to appreciate pink much more than I ever have before."

Chapter Twenty One

Candy

BY THE TIME CANDY and Votra arrived at the launch party, the venue was packed.

The ballroom was magnificent, with several large, sparkling crystal chandeliers hanging from the coffered ceiling. Elegant pillars with gilded trim flanked the massive entrance archway.

Clusters of people dotted the room; some standing against the walls, others occupying the section of tables that was thankfully much smaller than what they'd started with. And they were all drinking. Waiters in crisp suits and bowties moved languidly throughout the room with trays of what looked like champagne in plastic flutes. The plastic was a little tacky, but Candy could get over it.

Xyxy was on them almost the second they walked in, brandishing two flutes and pressing them into Candy's and Votra's hands. She looked incredible in a square-necked navy blue dress that clung to her hips and kissed her knees, two loose tendrils of long hair framing her angular face. "Okay, my loves. Everyone is having a great time. People are testing out the app and they're *obsessed*. I can't get people to actually get *out* of the virtual reality rooms so other people can take a turn."

Candy grinned, her heart pounding wildly. "Thank you so, so much," she breathed, pulling Xyxy in for an embrace with her free arm. "Everything looks amazing. Thank you so much for taking care of this for us."

"Oh, trust me, this was nothing." She waved Candy off with a crimson-nailed hand. "If I can get a bunch of sweaty wrestlers to be in the same place at the same time, I can *definitely* handle this." She brushed her lips across Candy's cheek, then pulled Votra in for a quick kiss, too. "Go mingle. Don't think for a *second* about stressing over anything."

One day, when Starcrossed made Candy rich, she was going to give Xyxy everything she'd ever desired. "Thank you so much, Xyxy," Votra said, and Xyxy gave her cheek an affectionate squeeze before dashing off to do God only knew what.

Candy tipped back her flute and drained it in one go. It didn't taste exactly like champagne, but it was bubbly and alcoholic, and that was all she needed. "Okay. Mingle. We can do that, right?"

Votra did the same, letting out a little gasp. "Alright, yes. We can. We should introduce ourselves to some of the users, right?"

"Probably–" Candy scanned the room for a second and her eyes fell upon a crown of white hair. For once, her uncle wasn't the tallest person in the room–Kratos's species could be pretty tall–but he was definitely still the tallest human. "My uncle's here. Can I introduce you?"

"I would love to meet him." They tossed their empty flutes into a bin by the door before Candy took Votra's hand, leading her towards her mountain of an uncle.

Luckily, it would be difficult to lose him in the crowd. He was a nearly seven foot tall human with skin as white as his hair; he stood out, even among the tallest aliens. "Uncle Lochlan!" she called out, lacing her fingers through Votra's as she practically dragged her through the crowd.

It took every iota of her self control to keep her cool, but the second he spoke, she dissolved into tears. "There's my Can-Can," he said, and Candy released Votra as he scooped her up into a bone-crushing hug.

That familiar citrusy, spicy smell of his cologne enveloped her. He smelled like home. "Hey, don't cry, kid. You're gonna screw up your makeup." He carefully set her back on the ground and offered her his handkerchief.

Candy laughed through her tears, wiping her eyes with it. "Too late." Lochlan rubbed at the corner of one of her eyes with his thumb, probably messing up her eyeliner but she couldn't even really bring herself to care. It had only been a couple of weeks since she'd seen him last, but she missed him.

She tucked his now eyeliner-coated handkerchief back into his pocket with a pat. He looked nice in his black blazer and muted red vest; she couldn't help but wonder if Vince had something to do with that. He'd even shaved, his face free of the stubble that always used to prickle Candy's face when she hugged him. The cuff links at

Lochlan's wrists bore metal sea serpent heads, which were so beautiful they could only be the work of Vincent Luque.

The man in question appeared beside Lochlan a few moments later, two flutes in hand. Vince was the complete antithesis of her uncle; a lithe, elegant Mexican man a little over twenty years Lochlan's junior with thick, feathery black hair that framed his elf-like features. Tonight, he was in a crushed velvet suit the color of sapphires, the shirt underneath a satin button down of the same color. A brooch with the same serpent head as Lochlan's was clasped on his lapel.

"Here, take this. You look like you need it," he said with a playful grin. While Lochlan hadn't even seemed to notice Votra standing awkwardly by Candy's side, Vince honed in on her immediately. "You must be Votra, right?"

Votra looked almost surprised to be spoken to. "I am, yes." Candy placed a supportive hand on the small of Votra's back.

Vince passed her the second glass. "It's so nice to meet you, Votra," Vince said, his voice sickly sweet. He fluttered his mascaraed eyelashes at Votra, reaching a small hand out to shake hers. "I hope our Candy hasn't given you too much trouble."

"Not at all. She is wonderful," Votra said, the tenderness in her voice making Candy's heart lurch. She itched to reach out and grab her hand, but she stopped herself.

Lochlan would be much easier to approach without the context that Candy and Votra were dating. He offered his hand to Votra for a handshake, his way of asserting dominance, but he let out a big, pleased laugh. "Damn, you got a handshake on you," he said, and Votra flushed with pride. *That's my girl.*

Vince's eyes were laser focused on Votra, and for a second, Candy thought she was maybe worrying about the wrong uncle. She knew he wasn't going to drill Votra with questions about their relationship, but she could venture a guess that he'd probably already seen right through them.

"Oh, I forgot to get myself a drink," Vince chirped, looping his arm through Candy's. "Come with me to the bar?"

Something told Candy she didn't have much choice. "Uh, sure." She shot a glance at Votra, who gave her a little smile. She'd be fine. Lochlan immediately launched into a barrage of questions as they walked away.

Vince fell into step beside Candy as they headed for the bar. "So you didn't wanna tell your uncle you're dating your boss, huh?"

Candy froze in her tracks. "How did you know?" she spluttered, giving his arm a shove.

"I hate to break it to you, but you literally couldn't be subtle if you tried. Neither of you. Votra looks at you like the sun shines out of your ass." But he gave Candy's arm an affectionate squeeze. "It's cute."

Candy sighed, giving in. "I just know Uncle Lochlan's gonna shake her down and she's already so high strung as it is. He can shake her down *after* the party, but just not right now."

"Heard, chef. I'll keep him on a leash, don't worry. But after the party, I'm not responsible for what comes out of that giant mouth of his."

That was what Candy was afraid of. Lochlan meant the best–he would probably love Votra immediately, but he was a bit like a bulldog at first. And her poor, anxious Votra definitely couldn't handle a bulldog tonight.

"I probably should have warned her, huh?" Candy asked, grimacing.

"Probably." He ordered a paloma from the bar–bless Xyxy's heart, she'd made sure the bar was stocked with plenty of Earth liquor. Candy could really go for a margarita right now. "She's sweet. Definitely not who I would have pegged as your type. I expected another greasy, weasely film bro."

"Hey, fuck you." But she grinned, her eyes falling on Votra again. She was easing into conversation with Lochlan, though she still looked profoundly uncomfortable. But she sure was trying. "I love her. A lot."

"I can tell." Vince took her free hand and squeezed it, and Candy's eyes immediately prickled with tears. "And she better be good to you, or I'll kick her ass."

"Yeah, yeah." She laughed softly, pulling him into a one-armed hug. "Thank you."

Candy and Votra broke away once Votra's social battery started to dwindle; she'd made it through a solid hour of conversation with Uncle Lochlan, which Candy had to say was pretty impressive. But she had to reserve some of that battery for talking to the people who were here for the app.

"I like your uncles," Votra said once they regrouped. "Lochlan is very... talkative."

Candy laughed so hard she nearly choked on her third flute of sparkling wine. "He sure is. He's where I get it from. But the fact that he talked so long is a good sign. That means he likes you."

"That is–" Something behind Candy caught Votra's eye, and she drained the rest of her glass. "Zeele is here."

Candy's mouth immediately ran dry. She guessed she shouldn't be surprised. Why wouldn't the owner of another dating app come to scope out the competition? "Where?"

"Over there. Speaking with your uncles."

Fuuuuuuck. Candy whipped around on her heel to see Lochlan and Vince, roped into conversation with a qintaril nearly as tall as Lochlan. She tried not to laugh at the fact that Vince did *not* look happy.

"Shit. Okay." Candy sucked in a sharp breath. "How do you wanna play this? We can ignore her if you want."

"No, we should speak with her. I have no doubt that she knows I am here, but she does not know about you. Her interacting with your uncles is, unfortunately, just bad luck."

Okay. Great. Candy was going to meet Votra's ex and she was going to have to be professional because this was the launch party for *their* app. The last thing they needed was negative social media attention because Candy started a fight with one of their competitors.

This was going to be fine. "Great. Let's go rescue my uncles. Vince looks like he's about to pop a blood vessel."

Candy's heart pounded in her ears as they approached Vince, Lochlan, and Zeele. Lochlan had completely tuned out, his green eyes glassy. Vince, however, was focused as ever, a slight scowl playing on his glossy lips.

"You know, I didn't have that experience with LoveNet," Vince was saying, folding his arms over his chest. "Have you thought about increasing that three hundred character limit?"

"Not particularly." Zeele's voice was smooth, polished like she'd stood in the mirror the night before and practiced each word. She swirled the drink in her flute before taking a small sip. "We did extensive surveying of our user base, and a very small percentage of users needed more than even a hundred characters."

"Sounds to me like they're using the app wrong." Vince's attention shifted to Candy and Votra, and Zeele's gaze followed his. She stiffened visibly, her eyes immediately landing on Votra.

"Votra. I wondered when I might run into you." She turned to Votra, not acknowledging Candy. This time, Candy didn't think twice about lacing her arm around Votra's protectively.

Zeele was beautiful in the way a snake was. Her eyes were much more narrow than Votra's, her skin a deep emerald green. Her face was slender, angular, almost threatening in itself. The suit she wore clung to her thin frame, her blouse clasped firmly at the base of her throat.

"Hello, Zeele." Every muscle fiber in Votra's body was clenched, but she remained composed. "I hope that you are having a good time."

"Oh, I am, thank you. I was just talking to Victor here about LoveNet."

"It's *Vince*," Vince interjected, voice dripping with agitation. "I was just telling her how much I really *didn't* like LoveNet, actually."

A smile quirked at the corner of Votra's lips, but she suppressed it. "Have you done any of the Starcrossed demos yet?"

"I have, actually. And I was impressed. You did a fantastic job, little Votra. I mean that." Zeele's words seemed genuine enough, but there was a hint of condescension to it that stoked the irritation simmering in Candy's stomach.

"It was a collaborative effort," Votra said. "Between Candy and I."

Zeele finally seemed to notice that Candy existed, her cat-like stare landing on her. "You hired someone? Incredible. I never thought I would see the day that you would ask for help. Good for you."

This was *really* starting to piss Candy off. "I'm sorry, I don't think we've properly met," Candy said, injecting as much saccharine sweetness into her voice as she could. "Who are you again?"

Zeele didn't miss a beat. "My name is Zeele." She whipped a business card from her pocket, offering it to Candy. "Founder of LoveNet. We were the number one ranked social app on the hypernet for three quarters of the last year."

Candy took the card, resisting the urge to jam it in Zeele's drink. "Oh, I'm familiar with LoveNet. Incredible app. I especially admire how you have to spend twenty credits a month to do more than send an emoji to ten people a day."

Zeele wasn't fazed. "You are too cute. No wonder Votra chose you to work with. The two of you will learn one day that this field is about making money where you can. You will never be able to survive off app creation if you give it all away for free. But Votra has heard this whole speech before, right, my dear?"

"I have. Many times." Votra's voice grew weaker, and she seemed to shrink into Candy's side. Candy rested a reassuring hand between Votra's shoulder blades, Zeele's sharp eyes following the movement.

"No offense, Zeele, because I'm sure your advice is absolutely riveting, but I think we have a pretty good handle on what we're going to do with Starcrossed. We're not really looking for advice," Candy said. Lochlan let out a low whistle; he must have tuned back in once the promise of a fight presented itself. "Thanks, though. Very generous of you to offer."

Zeele's lips turned up into an unkind smile. "Of course. It is not my business how you decide to run yours, even if you are doing yourselves a great disservice." She looked back to Votra one last time. "It has been lovely to see you again, Votra. Though I feel like I must remind you, in case you have forgotten, that you did not want to date someone you worked with again. You made that quite clear to me the last time I saw you."

"Well dating someone you work with generally works out better when one of you isn't a *thieving cunt*," Candy snapped. From somewhere beside her, Vince gasped. "Good luck riding off all the work Votra gave you. Eventually, you're gonna have to come up with your own shit, and then you'll *really* be in trouble."

Finally, the unshakable Zeele was shaken. Even Votra shot her a look that she refused to acknowledge for the moment. "I... need to take a call. If you will excuse me."

The moment she was out of earshot, Vince erupted into laughter. "Holy shit, Candy, that was *brutal*," he said, wiping a tear from his eye. Lochlan still seemed to be reeling–his poor old brain was processing a lot of new information.

"Candy," Votra murmured, just quiet enough that only Candy could hear. "Can I speak with you? Alone?"

Shit. She'd gotten ahead of herself. Zeele was going to tell everyone that the co-owner of Starcrossed was a crazy, unhinged bitch that attacked her, unprovoked. "Uh, be right back," Candy said to her uncles. She let Votra guide her out of the ballroom and into the quieter, open hallway of the hotel.

"I'm so sorry, I–"

And then Votra kissed her harder than she'd ever kissed her before.

Chapter Twenty Two

Votra

VOTRA HAD PREPARED HERSELF all day for seeing Zeele; it was bound to happen. But selfishly, she hadn't considered what it might be like for Candy to see her.

Obviously, she had nothing to worry about. She should have been more worried about Zeele instead. Votra sure as hell wouldn't have wanted to be on the receiving end of Candy's ire.

"That was amazing," Votra managed between feverish kisses. "You... *you* are amazing."

Candy's body sagged with relief. "Thank God. I thought you were gonna be mad at me. I was trying so hard to be professional, but she's such a fucking *bitch*."

That was hard to disagree with. But Votra had never had the nerve to stand up for herself.

"You did everything right, I promise." All Votra wanted to do right now was rip this gorgeous dress off Candy and show her just how grateful she was. But they had a crowd to address.

Candy gave her a soft smile, her hands resting on either side of Votra's face. "Good. Because if I ever see that cunt again, she'll be getting a *lot* worse than that."

"Gods help her." Votra took Candy's hands in her own, drawing them to her lips. "I love you, my *ta'qel*. My heart."

Candy's eyes watered, and she gave Votra's hands a little squeeze. "I love you, too."

The door behind them creaked open, a blue head popping out. "Ugh, thank fuck, there you two are." Xyxy closed the door carefully behind her. "Everything okay?"

"Never better." Candy grinned. "Is it time for us?"

"Sure is." She threw her arms around both of their shoulders, pulling them in close to her. "I'm so proud of both of you."

Emotion threatened to close Votra's throat, but she took a deep breath. This was it. She could handle one speech, especially if Candy was there with her.

Xyxy hurried to the stage ahead of them, Candy and Votra lingering at the foot of it while she introduced them. "Hey, everyone! If I can have your attention for just a few minutes!" Xyxy said into the microphone, her voice filtering throughout the room. "I hope everyone's having fun so far!" The crowd answered with enthusiastic cheers that made Votra's heart skip. "The Starcrossed team has a few words they'd like to say to you all, so please, give them your undivided attention!"

Candy and Votra strode onto stage to a chorus of raucous cheers. Candy's uncles were particularly loud, Lochlan's hands cupped around his mouth as he shouted.

Votra guided Candy to the microphone by the small of her back. Candy glanced back at her, and Votra mouthed 'go ahead.' She had just as much right to a speech as Votra did, and Votra didn't particularly want to go first.

Candy wrapped her hand around the microphone, an easy smile spreading across her lips. "Hi everyone. Thanks so much for coming to our launch party. I can't put into words just how much it means to us." Her voice was already thick with tears, and she laughed, moving her mouth away from the microphone as she did. "Sorry. I knew I was gonna cry up here. This whole experience has meant the world to me. It has been so fun and so fulfilling to be a part of making the dating app that I always wished existed. So many of the apps out there aren't very inclusive and still subscribe to outdated ideals of dating. Some of them make you pay to talk to more than one person in a day."

Votra suppressed a snort. Gods, she loved this woman.

"But with Starcrossed, we wanted to make an app that everyone could use, without asking people to spend their hard-earned money to possibly meet the love of their life. We wanted to make an app where everyone feels safe and seen, regardless of sexuality, gender, species, or that one really specific dealbreaker you have that no one understands." A hum of polite laughter erupted from the crowd. "Anyway. I hope you all love the app as much as I do. I wanna turn things over to Votra, the real mastermind behind this whole thing. This app is *her* baby." She shot Votra a grin, and suddenly, all of her nerves melted away.

She knew exactly how she wanted to do this. Votra took to the microphone, raising it on its stand. "Thank you, Candy," she said, her eyes lingering on Candy for a little bit too long. "Hello, everyone. As Candy said, my name is Votra, and I am the founder of Starcrossed. I hope that I will not bore you with my speech, as my partner here is definitely the more charismatic one of us." The crowd laughed once again, and Votra's eyes fell quickly on the two people she was looking for. Qaed and Vendi stood side by side, not too far from Candy's family. Qaed winked at Votra, and her chest felt just a little less tight.

"I have been working on iterations of Starcrossed for years now and it has changed so much from its original mockups. But my ideals have never changed. I have always wanted Starcrossed to be as inclusive as possible, and I have always wanted it to be accessible. I want everyone in this room to be able to download the app and to immediately start using it as they see fit. I am incredibly proud of the product that we are putting out today, and I hope that you all are enjoying it as much as we enjoyed creating it."

Votra turned her attention to Candy, holding a hand out to her. Her pink brows furrowed, and Votra nodded at her. She hadn't put that much thought into her speech–she knew the motions, she knew what the crowd was going to expect of her.

But this was the most important part. She'd spent too much of their time together pretending that Candy didn't mean as much to her as she did. She'd hid her feelings for Candy like she was ashamed of them.

And all she wanted to do now was scream them from the rooftops. A stage would have to do.

Candy placed her hand and her trust in Votra's, and Votra wrapped her other hand around their joined ones. "I have one last thing I would like to say, and I believe it is the most important one." Votra squeezed Candy's hand. "If it is at all any testament to the matchmaking power of our app... I hired Candy to help me finish the app. Our relationship was purely business–but I suppose spending twelve hours a day with someone, talking about nothing but love, will shift the dynamic a bit." The grin on Vendi's face encouraged her to continue. "Over the course of building the app, I was lucky enough to get to know her and to allow her to get to know me. She has changed my life in more ways than I can count and in ways that I did not think my life would ever change. I, and Starcrossed, would not be what we are today if I had never met her."

She turned to Candy then, and it was as if the rest of the world had melted away around them. Nothing else mattered anymore. She rested her free hand on Candy's wet cheek, Candy's tear-filled eyes meeting hers. "I love you, Candy Murdock. Thank you for bringing your chaotic energy and infallibly huge heart into my life. I am a better person for it."

"I can't believe you brought me on stage just to make me cry in front of everyone," Candy said, her words wobbly.

Votra leaned down and kissed her, and she never wanted to stop. The crowd erupted into wild cheers and whistles, and Candy snaked an arm around Votra, pulling her closer.

She wished this exact moment could last forever. But Candy pulled away from the kiss entirely too fast, her eyes glued on Votra. The way she was looking at her, with those adorable flushed cheeks, sparkling eyes and shy smile, made Votra want to steal her away and forget about the party completely.

Candy's grip didn't move from Votra's, but she moved closer to the microphone, tilting it down so that she could speak into it. "Sorry we stole the 'first Starcrossed couple' title. Guess that was kinda unfair. Enjoy the party, everyone!" The crowd gave one last cheer before Candy led them off the stage.

Candy rested a hand on the nape of Votra's neck, tugging her down to her level. Her lips brushed across Votra's ear, sending a shiver down her spine. "I hope you're ready for tonight, because after *that,* I'm not letting you leave the bed until you come so hard you can't walk," she whispered as quietly as she possibly could, and Votra stiffened in every sense of the word. Gods, she *really* didn't want to walk around here with a hard on.

"I will hold you to that," Votra murmured, pressing a benign kiss to the corner of Candy's glossy lips.

Vendi and Qaed found them shortly after, and Votra had to pretend like her heart wasn't pounding aggressively against her ribs. "It is about damn time," Qaed said, enveloping Candy in a hug first. "Vendi, those fifty credits, please."

"For the record, we made this bet before I met Candy." Vendi stared at Votra, but immediately hugged her. "I am happy for you, *zi'qal.* I have not seen you this happy in a long time."

Votra wasn't sure she'd *ever* felt this happy. Certainly never with Zeele, and probably not before her, either. "Thank you, Vendi," Votra said softly, tears choking her words.

Most of their night after that was filled with congratulations, and one shocked outburst from Lochlan. "You two are *dating?*" he'd blanched, followed by a smug smirk from Vince. He'd tried to assault Votra with even *more* questions about her life, but Candy mercifully saved her with the promise that he could interrogate her later.

They flitted around the room, engaging in conversation with users of the app. Candy placed herself at the head of each conversation, Votra's attention and social battery draining. All she wanted to do was escape; she needed a solid week of zero interactions to recover.

But it seemed that her speech had worked. People were using the app, and they spoke with a few users who had made matches at the party.

Starcrossed was real. It was out there, and people were using it. And they *liked* it.

Votra was just beginning to get overwhelmed when Candy finally gave her the 'let's get out of here,' and she couldn't agree fast enough. Candy led Votra out of the ballroom and into the lobby of the hotel, which was mercifully quieter.

"God, I need to sleep for a thousand years," Candy groaned, leaning all of her body weight on Votra. She rested her hands on Votra's chest. "I have a proposition for you."

If this was anything like her last proposition, Votra couldn't envision herself saying no. "Yes?"

"Let's get a hotel room. We're already here, and... this is a *nice* hotel. You deserve a nice hotel room." Candy's eyes flashed with something wicked, and Votra's flesh prickled with excitement.

"I like the idea of that."

Epilogue

Candy

BROOKLYN FELT MUCH COLDER this winter–or maybe Candy was so used to being so warm back on Veterok-III that it made New York feel like an arctic tundra.

Votra didn't seem terribly bothered by it. She'd chosen to leave her coat at the Murdock house, despite Candy's dad's nagging. He'd loved Votra from the second she walked through the door, and the thought of his new favorite daughter walking the streets of Brooklyn in December without a coat nearly did his head in.

"Sorry about them," Candy said as they walked down the snowy street. Pillow-soft snow fluttered around them, the snow salt crunching under their boots as they walked. "Especially Dad. He's trying to impress you, in his dorky way."

"I like him." Votra looped her arm through Candy's, providing her a little more support in the unforgiving terrain. "Sometimes, it is nice to be fussed over by a parent."

Candy leaned her head against Votra's upper arm. "You're practically his daughter now. You know that, right? He's gonna be calling you 24/7, so get ready for that."

"I would not mind that." Votra's eyes sparkled with genuine fondness, and Candy was pretty sure that, if her heart swelled any more, it would just explode out of her chest. She'd had no doubt in her mind that her parents would love Votra, but seeing it filled her with a joy that she didn't know existed.

Their target for the day was a coffee shop that Candy had frequented during college called Brewed Awakening. The shop shone brightly on the corner of her street, its yellow awning and twinkling fairy lights laced around the fence beckoning them. Candy couldn't wait to sink her teeth into one of their cardamom cinnamon rolls.

The bell hanging above the door chimed as they walked in, the aroma of freshly roasted coffee beans and warm spices welcoming them. It was just as cozy as Candy remembered it.

Midday was always the best time to come; the morning rush of impatient New York businessmen was far behind them, and now the only people who lingered were NYU students and the occasional gaggle of older women. They had their pick of the mismatched collection of sofas and armchairs in the dining area.

Candy clung to Votra as they waited in line, her alien girlfriend's eyes wide as saucers as they raked over the display case of glimmering, fat pastries. She'd definitely adjusted to eating the food on Veterok-III, and had actually started to prefer some of it to Earth food, but she was excited to return to something that had been a creature comfort for her.

After a barrage of 'what is that?'s from Votra as she pointed out different pastries in the case, they approached the register. A familiar face peered at them through wide tortoise shell glasses. "Candy?"

Candy immediately peeled away from Votra, all of her breath leaving her body in a surprised gasp. "Oh my God! Clement! You still work here?" He rounded the counter and scooped Candy into a tight hug.

Honestly, the only way she even knew it was Clement was because he was the only person who worked here that would recognize her. He'd changed so much in the probably two years since she'd seen him—she'd pulled back a little when things with Ross started to get bad, and she hadn't really told many people when she moved to Veterok-III. His hair wasn't clipped short to his head anymore; it fell about his round, kind face in waves, dusting his shoulders. His features had become much more pronounced, his brow stronger, his jaw, while still soft, much more angular now than it was before.

And he had facial hair! "Please don't remind me," he said in a deadpan, pulling back and resting his hands on her shoulders. He was still a victim to cable knit sweaters, Candy noticed. Only Clement Hall would pull them off as well as he did. "How have you been? I mean, gosh, you look incredible."

"I'm good! I, uh, moved out of the galaxy." She gave a sheepish grin. "And I have a girlfriend."

Clement's shoulders slumped with relief. "Thank God you got rid of him. No offense."

Clement was one of the few friends Candy had that wasn't silent about his opinion about Ross–she hadn't appreciated it at the time, but he had been infuriatingly right. She just wished she'd listened to him sooner. His big brown eyes moved over to Votra, whose eyes were still glued to the pastry case. "That's her? With the horns?"

"Yep. Isn't she hot?" Candy grinned so hard her cheeks hurt.

"For a girl, sure." Clement winked. "Hey, I should get this line down a little, but if you're still around in an hour or two, I'm gonna take my break and we can catch up a little."

Judging by the way Votra was eye fucking the display case, Candy was pretty sure they weren't going anywhere any time soon. "Trust me, we'll be here."

Clement returned to the register and Candy proceeded to order one of everything Votra laid her eyes on for even a second. She ordered a mocha for herself and a coffee and a hot chocolate for Votra–she couldn't decide which one she wanted more–and recruited her much stronger girlfriend to carry their tray of spoils to a plush leather couch in the corner of the shop.

"That was Clement," Candy said as Votra settled the tray of goodies on the coffee table in front of them. "We were really good friends in college. I haven't seen him in *years*. He's gonna come over here in a little bit and I'll properly introduce you to him. I think you'd like him."

"I apologize that I did not introduce myself while you were talking," Votra said. "I was... a bit distracted."

"Cupcake, I know you were." Candy placed her hand lovingly on Votra's knee. "That's why I just spent, like, a hundred dollars on pastries."

"You say that as if you are not going to partake in them as well."

"Oh, I *will* be. I love partaking."

Votra smiled, taking Candy's hand from her knee and drawing it to her lips. "Thank you for taking the time to show me around your planet. Earth is... very different from what I have seen in vids."

"You mean dirtier?" Candy snorted, letting Votra take her slice of chocolate cake before grabbing a ham and cheese croissant for herself. Votra wasn't so interested in the savory ones. "New York has its gross parts, but it's also really pretty sometimes. Like right now. I'm glad you got to see the snow."

"It reminds me of Alqen, in a way," Votra said through a mouthful of cake. Candy didn't think she'd ever met someone who loved chocolate quite as much as Votra did. "The way the sun reflects off the snow. It is quite lovely."

Warmth blossomed in Candy's chest, and it wasn't from the sip of mocha she took. "Thank you for coming with me. I know you've gotten kind of a lot from me lately, between meeting my uncles and now my parents and my sister. But they all loved you. Especially my sister." Cori had practically trapped Votra in conversation, asking her about Kratos, about colleges–she'd just made up her mind to go to college in space, and she figured, who better to ask than a native?–and Votra had taken it in stride.

"I enjoyed it. I promise."

They gradually made their way through maybe half of the pastries, Votra taking on more of them than Candy, and Candy let herself bask in the warm glow of the dim coffee shop lighting. The homesickness had certainly gotten easier to handle the longer she was in Kratos, but she also found herself wishing this moment would never end. Votra was here, she was only a few blocks away from her family, and she was surrounded by pastries.

Clement came over about half an hour later, giving the two a little wave. "Is it still okay if I join you for a bit?" he asked.

"Of course!" Candy chirped, patting the couch next to her. "Hungry? We have so many pastries left."

"Oh, I'm good, thanks. I've had all of these things so many times, I can hardly look at them."

Candy shifted a little, taking one of Votra's hands in hers. "Clement, this is my girlfriend, Votra. Votra, this is Clement."

Clement's eyes went wide as he took Votra in. "Wow. Sorry, you're just... really pretty," he said, a blush creeping onto Votra's cheeks. "It's really nice to meet you."

"You as well," Votra said shyly, burying her face in her mug of hot chocolate.

Clement leaned in closer to Candy. "Does she have a single brother?" he stage-whispered, and Candy snorted.

Votra answered before Candy could. "Oh, I do, actually–"

"No, no. Do *not* set my sweet Clement up with Qaed. He's a menace," Candy interjected, and Votra laughed. "He probably *would* be your type though."

"What's that supposed to mean?"

"He's kind of a whore. But like, a nice one. He's not the type to like, ditch you in the middle of the night, but he's probably gonna send you that 'thanks for last night but let's not do it again' text."

"Yeah, you're right. Exactly my type." Clement huffed, snatching the almond croissant from Candy's hand and taking a bite.

"Some things never change." Candy gave Clement's back a gentle rub. "So how are things with you, anyway? How's your mom?"

She felt Clement stiffen under her hand. "She... passed away last month."

Shit. "Clem, I'm so sorry."

"It's okay." He stuffed entirely too much of the croissant into his mouth, and Candy could just barely make out the tears gathering at the corners of his eyes behind his glasses.

Clement wasn't always very upfront about his life, but the one thing Candy knew was that he was his mom's caretaker and had been for as long as she'd known him. Votra looked viscerally uncomfortable, and Candy immediately felt bad for dragging her into this. The poor thing was probably never gonna want to come back to Earth again.

"I think the thing that's been the hardest to adjust to is that I have no fucking clue what to do with myself anymore." He leaned into Candy's touch a little, and she continued rubbing soothing circles on his back, despite the fact that his warm sweater was practically giving her rug burn. "I just come here, and... go home. To no one. Cecily moved out, so it's literally just me in that big ol' house."

"Cecily moved out?" Cecily was Clement's twin sister, the more spontaneous, outgoing one of the two.

"Yeah. Her career took off and she's going on *tours* now. She's a whole adult now." Votra wordlessly offered him a chocolate glazed donut, and he took it, jamming it into his mouth. "And I still work *here*."

Woof. She'd hit a nerve for sure. "What do you want to do?" Votra asked gently.

"I don't know. I never really had the time to think about it." His words were muffled by donut, his mouth smeared with frosting. Votra handed him a napkin.

Candy pursed her lips. "You know, a very wise person once told me that if you're feeling stuck, you should just move out to space."

"You mean *you?*"

"Duh. I'm a very wise person. And as you can see, it has worked out *amazingly* for me."

Clement swallowed hard, choking a little around the too-large bite he'd taken. Votra offered him her coffee, and Candy couldn't help but smile at how kind her girlfriend was. Clement took a hearty sip to wash down the donut that threatened to choke him.

"I dunno, Candy. I'd be away from Cecily, and what if she needs me?" Clement reached for another pastry, but Candy smacked his hand away. The last thing she needed was to do the Heimlich on him.

Candy stopped her motions on Clement's back, resting a hand on his shoulder instead. "She's out there traveling the world. You just said that. She is *more* than fine. I can guarantee she has a million people here looking out for her."

Clement seemed to mull that over for a moment. "I guess you're right...."

"Oh! Qaed needs a roommate now that you've moved out, right, sweetie?" Candy clapped her hands together excitedly.

"I thought you just said Qaed was a menace and I should stay away from him."

"Well, he is a good roommate," Votra said. "He is a very tidy person. And it helps that he is almost never home."

Candy could practically see Clement's mind churning. She'd never known Clement to do anything for himself, and if there was anything Candy had learned about sending herself out into space, it was that it was the best thing she could have possibly done for herself.

"Think about it. You need a change, babe. You *deserve* one." Candy placed a hand on one side of Clement's head and pulled his head closer to her, planting a kiss on his temple. "Just shoot me a message and I'll get you into space ASAP."

Clement chewed his thumbnail thoughtfully. His nails were painted a cute, sunshine yellow color that really suited him. "I... should go for it, shouldn't I?"

Yes. Candy was so good at this. She deserved some kind of award for coming back to Earth and changing lives, one barista at a time. "I think you should. But if you need to take some time to think—"

"If I take any time to think about it, I'll back out." Clement's back straightened. "I wanna move to space."

Candy squealed, throwing her arms around him. "Yay! Okay, we're still here for a few days but I'm gonna get some stuff together. We'll figure this out, okay?"

"Please tell me I'm not gonna regret this," Clement muttered into Candy's sleeve.

"I promise, you're not." She pulled away, practically hopping to her feet. "I'm gonna get with Qaed about you moving in with him, and I'll text you later?"

Clement stood too, passing Candy the nearly empty box of pastries. "Sounds good. I'm off in four hours, so... if you need to call me, you can."

"Amazing!" Candy sang. "This is gonna be so great! Okay, I'll call you!" She threw her free arm around him again and squeezed.

This was going to be good for him, she could tell. She reached her hand out to Votra. "Ready to go, honey?"

Votra placed her hand in Candy's and stood, dusting the crumbs from her pants. "Yes." She glanced at Clement, who had scurried back to his place behind the register. "Are you certain this is a good idea? He and Qaed are... very different."

"Like you said, Qaed's never home. They'll be fine." Candy brushed a smear of powdered sugar from the corner of Votra's lips. "Let's go break the news to him that he's got a roommate."

Acknowledgements

As I'm writing this, it still hasn't entirely sunken in that my book is in the hands of you, my reader. So above all, I thank you. Thank you for taking a chance on me, on my girls, on my silly little alien romance.

Thank you to my earliest beta readers, Lulu, Melissa, and Lyra, who gave me the perfect combination of critical feedback and cheerleading and made me realize that maybe this book was worth putting out there. Thank you all for your continued support.

Thank you to the gay people in my phone, the discord server that gives me encouragement every single day and keeps me going. A special thanks to King and Elliot, who have both brought me to tears with their kind words about my book.

Thank you Laika, Felicette, and Veterok. I'm sorry that we failed you.

I would be remiss not to mention my spouse, Ash. Candy and Votra would not be who they are without all of our late night car rides, coffee shop dates, nights staying up way too late talking about our characters. I love you forever. Marry me again?

www.ingramcontent.com/pod-product-compliance
Lightning Source LLC
Chambersburg PA
CBHW050340110726
47899CB00007B/2571